Lock Down Publications and Ca$h Presents

OPPS CRY TOO

PART 3

BLOOD AND VENGEANCE

Written By

SAYNOMORE

First Edition 2025

Printed in the United States of America

This is a work of fiction. Names, characters, places, and incidents either are products of the author's imagination or are used fictitiously. Any similarity to actual events or locales or persons, living or dead, is entirely coincidental.

Lock Down Publications
P.O. Box 944
Stockbridge, GA 30281
www.lockdownpublications.com

Like our page on Facebook: Lock Down Publications
www.facebook.com/lockdownpublications.ldp

Stay Connected with Us!

Text **LOCKDOWN** to 22828 to stay up-to-date with new releases, sneak peaks, contests and more…

Like our page on Facebook:
Lock Down Publications

Join Lock Down Publications/The New Era Reading Group

Visit our website:
www.lockdownpublications.com

Follow us on Instagram:
Lock Down Publications

Email Us: We want to hear from you!

Prologue

Cash walked into the room, the air thick with the scent of chemicals and sweat. Four tables lined the center, each stacked with fifty kilos of pristine white powder, two hundred kilos in total. Sixteen females moved around the tables, stripping down and breaking the kilos into neat packages with precise, practiced motions.

Big Apple stepped up behind Cash, his eyes scanning the room. He didn't flinch. His eyes locked onto Cash's, sharp and calculated.

"It's been a few weeks now," Big Apple said, his voice low, almost casual, "and we took over the city. What are we gonna do now?"

Cash paused, letting the question hang in the thick, tense air. The girls worked silently, the only sound the soft crinkle of plastic and the occasional thump of a kilo hitting the table.

Cash's jaw tightened. He looked over the tables, the weight of power heavy in the room. "We keep moving," he said finally, voice steady. "We expand. We hit harder. Make sure nobody forgets who's running this city."

Big Apple nodded slowly, a small grin forming. "Then let's get to work. But first, what was it you said you had to show me that you said needs to be taken care of right now?"

Cash led Big Apple down the narrow staircase into the basement. The air grew thick, damp, with each step echoing off the concrete walls. At the bottom, dim light revealed three men tied up, hands bound behind their backs, bags over their heads.

"They're soldiers of Snake Eyes," Cash said, calm, but deadly. But his eyes burned with irritation, a predator sizing up prey. "The bastard's been getting under my skin. Thought it was time he learned what happens when you swim with sharks."

Big Apple's lips curled into a small grin. His fists clenched at his sides— not from fear, but anger and hate. He didn't flinch. He didn't hesitate. He was ready.

Cash opened a drawer and pulled out a hammer, the cold steel gleaming under the flickering light. Symone emerged from the shadows, P90 in hand, ready. But Big Apple didn't need a gun; his presence was enough to make the air tense. He stepped forward beside Cash, cracking his neck casually, like he'd been waiting for this moment.

"Let's remind them who's running this city," Big Apple said, his voice low, almost a growl.

Cash pulled the first bag off the tied man. The man's eyes went wide with terror.

Big Apple stepped closer, circling him like a wolf, eyes cold. "You talk too much," he said, calm, deadly. Then he delivered a hard punch to the man's stomach, bending him forward.

Cash followed with the hammer, and the first man's scream cut through the basement like glass.

Big Apple didn't wait. Instead, he leaned in, whispering, "You think Snake Eyes can save you? Not today." Then he grabbed the second man by the collar, pulling him up so Cash could strike. Each blow was precise, brutal. Big Apple's grin never left his face, his eyes gleaming with a dangerous thrill.

By the third man, Big Apple was fully in the moment, circling him, a predator enjoying the hunt. The man begged, pleading, trying to bargain for his life.

Big Apple's hand shot out, slamming the man against the table. "Shut up," he said, almost laughing. "You're about to learn a lesson."

Cash swung the hammer again, relentless.

Symone's P90 scanned the room, but it was almost unnecessary. The two men standing over their prey commanded absolute control.

Big Apple even leaned over one victim after the strike, whispering, "Tell Snake Eyes… tell him exactly who rules now."

The basement was alive with the sound of broken bone, screams, and the heavy breathing of predators at work. Big Apple didn't look away, didn't flinch, and he didn't hesitate. He delivered a swift kick to a man trying to curl in pain, forcing him to stay upright while Cash landed another crushing blow.

After it was over, Big Apple stepped back, hands on his hips, looking around the room with a grim satisfaction. "Yeah," he said, voice steady. "That'll get his attention."

Cash nodded, hammer still in hand, a satisfied grin on his face. "Loud and clear. Snake Eyes won't forget this."

Big Apple picked up one of the spilled bags of cocaine from the table, flicked it casually, and said, "Let him come. We're ready."

Symone lowered her P90, shaking her head slightly at the both of them, but even she couldn't deny the power in the room. Big Apple and Cash were untouchable, predators feeding on fear and control.

They walked back up the stairs, leaving a basement drenched in chaos, knowing the city now belonged to them. And when Snake Eyes found out… he'd learn the hard way.

Chapter 1

The streets of Queens were quiet for a reason. The calm before the storm. Symone's car slid silently down the empty avenues, the dark interior lit only by the dashboard's glow. In the backseat, wrapped in black plastic bags, were pieces of the men who had dared cross Cash. Soldiers of Snake Eyes, now just a message.

Symone's eyes were sharp. She was on point. Every turn, every stoplight, every corner she passed brought them closer to their destination. Tonight, the city would remember who ruled the streets.

By the time she arrived on Snake Eyes' turf, the sun had disappeared behind the city skyline, leaving the streets in shadow. She pulled the car into an alley and climbed out, plastic bags in hand. The streets were silent, but for those who lived there, even the smallest sound could echo. Symone moved with silence, placing the bags in strategic locations on stoops, against streetlamps, in doorways so that everyone would see. Everyone would understand.

Each placement was deliberate. One bag left on the stoop of a corner store, another on the steps of a rundown apartment, a third in the entrance to a vacant lot. She didn't just scatter them; she displayed them like trophies, a warning, a challenge.

Symone stepped back and looked at her work. The message was clear: Cash was coming, and anyone who crossed him would pay. She got back in the car, leaving the neighborhood quietly. Every shadow seemed alive, as if the streets themselves were holding their breath. Snake Eyes was in his penthouse, the city sprawled below him like a living map. His phone buzzed. A single text: *"We know what you did. Cash sends his regards."* Attached was a grainy photo of one of the bags, the blood dark against the concrete.

Snake Eyes froze. Rage coursed through him, sharp and raw. He knew immediately who was behind this. Cash. The name hit him like a punch to the gut. Not the men he could replace them but the message, the audacity, the total disregard for his authority… that was personal.

He slammed the phone down on the desk, his fists shaking. Around him, his soldiers waited, tense, silent. They'd seen the city shift under Cash's influence, but this… this was war. A spark ignited in Snake Eyes' chest, burning hotter with every second.

"You see what happens when you cross him?" he growled, pacing. "He's marking territory. Telling everyone who runs these streets now. But we'll show him…"

A soldier stepped forward, hesitant. "Boss… what do you want us to do?"

Snake Eyes turned slowly, eyes dark, filled with hate. "We hunt them," he said, voice low and dangerous. "Every street. Every corner. We make him pay for every ounce of blood spilled. And we'll start with Cash."

Outside, the city didn't yet know that war had been declared. But by morning, the streets would be on fire, whispers of violence spreading faster than the sun. Symone's display was more than a warning it was a declaration.

Snake Eyes grabbed a rifle off the wall, slamming it into his hands with a metallic clang. "I want them scared. I want the city shaking," he barked at his men. "Cash thinks he owns Queens… we'll remind him who the real fucking king is."

Down in the streets, the people saw the bags, felt the chill of fear running down their spines. The whispers started immediately.

"Did you see this?"

"Bodies in the streets!"

"Cash did this. Cash is taking over."

Every block became a rumor, every alley a story.

Symone drove away, satisfied. She didn't need applause. The fear, the shock, the city waking up to the reality of Cash's rule that was her reward. in the dark corners of Queens, Snake Eyes was already plotting on the way he was going to body cash and anyone who stood next to him.

***

Rain hammered the streets of New York like a drumbeat for the city's chaos, slicking the asphalt and making the neon signs bleed into puddles. Inside the high-rise apartment, the hum of the city was a distant roar, swallowed by the low ceiling and the smell of smoke. Cash leaned against the rain-streaked window, a blunt perched between his fingers. He took a long drag, eyes tracing the people moving like shadows below, waiting.

"Did you drop the bags?" His voice was calm. Too calm. A predator's patience hiding the storm beneath.

Symone nodded. She moved with the kind of confidence only hardened streets and dangerous alliances could teach. Sliding onto the chair across from him, she let her eyes lock on his, unwavering. "Yeah," she said, voice steady but with an edge that carried weight. "Just like you told me. But we gotta be on point. Snake Eyes… he's dangerous. He might have enough heart left to come after us."

Cash turned from the window, smoke curling around his face like a halo of menace. He smirked, a slow, almost casual twist of lips that made the threat in his next words sharper than any knife. "Good," he said, voice low and deliberate. "Because next time… he'll be burying his mother."

Symone's eyes narrowed, reading him. Not the casual threat of a street-level thug, but the calm of a man who had already seen what he was capable of and had no hesitation to act. The room felt smaller suddenly, filled with the weight of intent, with the rain outside drumming like war drums on the city.

"You sure about this, Cash?" she asked, leaning forward, voice softer but laced with steel. "He's not a man you can scare with words. You think he'll back down?"

Cash laughed, a low, dangerous rumble that didn't reach his eyes. He flicked the ash from the blunt, watching it fall into the tray like tiny sparks of warning. "He doesn't get to back down, Symone. Not from me. Not ever. Every time he thinks he's safe, he's wrong. That's the way it's always been. That's the way it'll stay."

Her hands rested on the table, fingers tapping against the wood, a rhythm that mirrored her thoughts calculated, precise, ready. She was dangerous too, but her kind of danger was measured. Cash's was raw, untamed, a storm in human form. She met his gaze, challenging and unwavering. "And if it goes south? If Snake Eyes actually fights back?"

Cash's eyes hardened. "Then it won't just be him. It'll be everyone who thought they could cross me. Every street, every corner, every man who ever looked at me like I was small. This isn't about Snake Eyes anymore. It's about setting the city straight. Making sure the next story they tell about me… is one that leaves them shitting themselves at night."

The room went quiet for a beat, only the rain outside filling the spaces between words. Symone's jaw clenched, but she didn't speak. She knew that feeling. That hunger. Cash had it in him like fire under ice cold, patient, but deadly once unleashed.

He took another drag from the blunt, blowing smoke slowly toward the ceiling. The haze curled, filling the room with tension thick enough to cut with a knife. "Symone," he said finally, softer now, almost intimate, "I need you sharp. Not just smart. Not just fast. I need you ready to do what has to be done, no matter what that means."

Her lips pressed together, the unspoken agreement passing between them. She was in. Always had been. Always would be. That wasn't loyalty, it was survival, and it was passion, and it was fire meeting fire.

"You got it," she said. "I'm on point. But Cash… this isn't a game. Snake Eyes… he doesn't play fair."

Cash smiled again, sharper this time, a predator's grin. "I don't either. You must have forgotten who the fuck I am and my body count, so I say get him. All you need to say is got him. You get what the fuck I'm saying, Symone?"

Symone nodded as she looked at him

He turned back to the window, watching the streets flood beneath the city lights. Every car, every shadow, every sound was a piece of the chessboard, and he was already five moves ahead. Symone watched him, the Intensity in his eyes like liquid steel. This wasn't fear. This was inevitability.

Outside, the rain began to slow, turning from a hammering storm to a steady drumbeat. But inside, the storm had only just begun. Cash crushed the blunt under his boot, grinding it into the ashtray, leaving nothing but the scent of smoke and intent.

"Tonight," he said, voice low and dangerous, "we set the tone. We remind every motherfucker in this city why they don't fuck with us. Snake Eyes? He's just the beginning."

Symone leaned back, letting the words sink in. She could feel the electricity in the room, the pulse of anticipation, the danger so close it felt like it could burn skin. She had worked with dangerous men before, but Cash… Cash wasn't just dangerous. He was legend in the making, a storm that didn't apologize.

"And you know," he continued, almost conversationally, "if Snake Eyes thinks he can come for me, he's gonna find out why I don't leave loose ends. And when it's over… he'll wish he'd never been born."

Symone's hand drifted to the table, tapping again, slower now, deliberate. She didn't need to speak. The message was clear, sharp as broken glass: Cash was ready. And if anyone crossed him, there would be no mercy.

The city outside continued to pulse, lights reflected in puddles like molten metal. Inside, two warriors sat, calm on the surface but roaring underneath, each heartbeat syncing with the other, each second a promise of the fire to come. Rain couldn't wash this away. The city couldn't drown it out. The storm inside this room inside these two was just beginning.

Cash finally leaned back, resting one shoulder against the wall. "We move tonight," he said, voice cutting through the quiet. "No mistakes. No hesitation. Snake Eyes… and everyone else in his path… they'll learn what happens when you fuck with me."

Symone nodded, eyes fierce. "No mistakes," she echoed. "I'm with you."

For a moment, they just sat, letting the tension hum, letting the city's pulse feed their own. Outside, the rain slowed, but inside, the fire burned hotter than ever. They weren't just planning they were promising. Blood would be spilled. Lines would be crossed. And when it was done, the streets would remember the names that dared to challenge them.

Cash smiled once more, the kind of smile that promised pain and victory in equal measure. "Good," he said. "Because next time… it's gonna be war. And we don't lose."

And with that, the storm inside the room finally matched the storm outside unstoppable, unrelenting, and ready to consume anyone foolish enough to stand in its way.

Chapter 2

The warehouse smelled of money, raw scent of paper, ink, and sweat. Humidity clung to the air from the endless stacks of bills being counted by workers hunched over metal tables. The snap-snap of rubber bands echoed like a drumbeat, sealing bundles of cash that ranged from grimy one-dollar bills to pristine hundreds that gleamed under the fluorescent lights.

K9 stood in the center of it all, his presence commanding without a word. He wasn't a man who needed to shout or wave his hands to be noticed. Just the way he carried himself the quiet confidence, the slow deliberate movements, the sharp eyes that missed nothing told everyone in the room who ran this empire. His tailored black sweatsuit contrasted with the workers in faded hoodies, and his gold watch caught the light every time he lifted his cigar.

Around the perimeter, security guards in dark tactical gear stood like statues, ARs strapped across their chests, eyes scanning every angle of the room. Nobody came in or out without being checked. Nobody spoke above a whisper unless K9 addressed them. The warehouse was his kingdom, and tonight, it was alive with money and power.

Stacks of bills rose like miniature skyscrapers across long wooden tables. Some were wrapped tight, others spilled loose, creating rivers of green. In the far corner, crates sealed shut carried unmarked merchandise whatever fueled the stream of cash that never seemed to stop.

K9's second-in-command, a sharp-eyed lieutenant named Darnell, stood beside him, hands clasped respectfully behind his back. Darnell had been with K9 long enough to know when to talk and when to stay silent. But tonight, the silence couldn't hold. His thoughts weighed heavy.

"Boss," Darnell began, his voice steady but low, "I been thinkin'… what's the real difference between Cash and Animal? They both killers. They both make moves. But I hear you speak on them different."

K9 exhaled a slow stream of smoke from his cigar, the cherry glowing red before dimming. His gaze traveled across the warehouse, watching the workers handle millions like it was nothing more than laundry. Then his eyes cut back to Darnell, sharp as a blade.

"Difference?" K9 repeated, his voice deep, unhurried, every word dipped in authority. "The difference is night and day. See… Cash is smart. He don't let his hunger blind him. He move different. He ruthless, no doubt cutthroat when he gotta be. But he loyal. He know his lane, and he stay in it. Cash don't need the spotlight. Don't crave attention. That's why I trust him."

Darnell nodded slowly, taking in every word.

K9 tapped ash into a silver tray, his tone hardening as he shifted. "Animal? He was the opposite. Greedy. Always wanted more than what was his. Wanted to be boss so bad, he forgot what it mean to be solid. For years, I knew he had that envy in his eyes. Thought he was bigger than me. Thought he was untouchable. But he poked the bear. And you already know what happens when you wake a bear out its sleep."

He paused, his voice carrying the weight of finality. "That's why he dead."

The words hung heavy in the air, more powerful than any threat. Workers nearby exchanged glances but kept their heads down, hands moving faster over the money, as if they feared even the stacks might hear.

Darnell glanced at the table nearest them where piles of bills overflowed into milk crates. His voice lowered further, cautious but curious. "Cash ain't playin', either. That move he just pulled… the way he laid out Snake Eyes' soldier, then sent the body parts across his turf like a message? That was brutal."

K9's lips curved into the faintest shadow of a smile. He didn't praise recklessness, but he respected precision. He leaned back in his leather chair one that looked almost out of place in the industrial warehouse yet fit him like a throne and rested the cigar between his fingers.

"That's exactly why I keep him close," K9 said. "He understand the rules. Snake Eyes need to learn the same. Cash gave him a warning. That's strategy. You can't buy that kind of instinct."

For a moment, silence returned. The only sounds were rubber bands snapping, bills shuffling, and the low hum of the ventilation. The warehouse felt alive, every corner breathing the rhythm of an empire.

K9 lowered his head, lit the cigar again, and inhaled deep. The glow lit up his sharp features skin smooth but eyes hardened by decades in the game. He wasn't old, but he carried himself like a man who had seen enough wars to know victory didn't belong to the loudest it belonged to the last one standing.

"Know who you dealin' with," K9 said finally, his voice deep, commanding, final. He leaned forward, eyes narrowing on Darnell. "That's the key. As long as it don't stop our money, let Cash have his fun. Let him show Snake Eyes what happen when you step where you don't belong. Just don't ever forget the empire comes first. Always."

Darnell nodded again, the respect in his eyes shining. He had no doubts this was more than a criminal operation. It was a machine. A system. And at the heart of it was K9, the quiet boss, the Black king who held the east Coast in a chokehold without the world even knowing his name.

The workers kept counting. The guards kept watching. And somewhere out in the city, Snake Eyes was plotting his revenge. But in that warehouse, with forty million in cash spread across tables and K9's words echoing like scripture, one thing was certain nobody moved without his blessing.

The war was coming. But tonight; money ruled.

***

The city never slept. Neon lights hummed over cracked sidewalks, cars honked two streets over, and the steady rhythm of hustlers moving on the block created a soundtrack of survival. The corner store on 116th had a line spilling out the door, and dice clattered against concrete while young men shouted bets over the noise. Nobody looked too hard at anything. In this part of the city, curiosity could get you killed.

Detective Cross walked with his hoodie pulled low, his jaw set tight, his eyes burning with a pain that had hollowed him out. Just days ago, he'd buried his wife and two kids. Their lives snuffed out in one brutal night because Big Apple had decided to "teach him a lesson." Cross replayed it every time he closed his eyes. The blood, the silence, the emptiness of his home. But tonight, grief had hardened into steel. Tonight, he wasn't just a detective. He was a man on a mission.

The block was buzzing with Big Apple's soldiers. Some leaned against cars, eyes sharp as they scanned for cops or rivals. Others huddled on stoops, selling poison to anyone with cash in hand. One worker in particular caught Cross's attention. A young hustler with a red fitted cap, standing at the corner with a small stack of cash, joking with another dealer. His body language said he was comfortable, untouchable. He had no idea his night was about to end.

Cross adjusted the gun in his waistband, feeling the weight press against his ribs. His pulse slowed. He had trained himself to never move emotional, but tonight was different. He wasn't going to lose control but he was going to make sure Big Apple felt the first ripple of what was coming.

He approached smooth, blending into the flow of pedestrians, just another hooded figure moving through the city. But as he got closer, his eyes never left the worker. He closed the gap fast. By the time the kid noticed, Cross was already on him, pressing cold steel against his side.

"Walk," Cross muttered, his voice low, dangerous.

The worker froze, his smile vanishing. "What the—"

"I said walk," Cross repeated, shoving him toward the narrow alley between two graffiti-tagged buildings. The young man stumbled forward, glancing around for help, but nobody looked his way. People kept moving eyes down, conversations flowing, dice rolling. In this neighborhood, you didn't see nothing unless you wanted trouble.

The alley smelled of piss, trash, and damp concrete. A flickering light bulb buzzed overhead, casting jagged shadows across the brick walls. Rats scattered as Cross pushed the worker deeper into the darkness, away from the street noise.

Cross pressed the barrel harder into the kid's waist, his eyes sharp, voice even. "I need to know where Big Apple's warehouses at. Where he keep the money. You tell me, you live. You don't you die right here."

The worker stiffened, fear creeping into his face, but his mouth twisted with bravado. "Man, fuck you. You don't scare me. Suck my meat."

For a second, silence filled the alley. Cross tilted his head, studying the kid's face. Then, a slow smile tugged at his lips not of amusement but of cold rage.

Without warning, Cross swung the gun across the worker's face. Crack! The impact echoed against the walls, blood spraying from the kid's busted lip as he stumbled and collapsed onto the filthy ground.

"You think this a game?" Cross growled, standing over him. The worker spat blood, trying to hold onto his pride, but fear was in his eyes now.

Cross crouched low, the gun inches from the worker's face. "You talk slick, huh? You got jokes? Suck on this."

And with that, Cross pulled the trigger. All you heard was the sound of the blast of the gunshot as Detective Cross shot the gun! The shots ripped through the alley, the muzzle flash lighting up the darkness. The worker's head snapped back, blood splattering against the brick wall. His body twitched once, then went still, eyes wide and unseeing.

Cross stood over him, chest rising and falling slowly, his expression cold. He didn't flinch. Didn't hesitate. His heart wasn't racing, it was steady, calm. The kind of calm that came when a man had already lost everything.

From the street, the sounds of dice games and arguments carried on, untouched by the violence just a few feet away. A woman pushing a stroller hurried past the mouth of the alley without turning her head. Two kids on bikes rode by, laughing, never noticing the body lying in the shadows. The city kept moving.

Cross wiped the gun's grip with his sleeve, his movements precise. He wasn't reckless. Revenge had to be smart. Every step had to be calculated. Big Apple had taken everything from him, and now he was going to dismantle him piece by piece. Tonight was only the beginning.

He stepped back out of the alley, blending into the crowd like nothing had happened. His hoodie still low, his hands in his pockets, his face unreadable. Behind him, the worker's lifeless body bled into the concrete, the echo of gunshots already swallowed by the city noise.

Nobody stopped him. Nobody asked questions. That was the way of the streets silence was survival.

Cross walked with purpose, his mind already moving to the next step. Big Apple thought he could break him. But what he didn't know was that he had awakened something worse than grief. He had awakened vengeance.

And vengeance walked quietly until it was ready to roar.

***

The night air over Harlem carried that restless hum of summer heat mixed with danger. Streetlights buzzed low and yellow, casting long shadows over cracked sidewalks and project walls tagged with names of soldiers who never made it home. On one of Cash's blocks, a fresh message had already been left behind—Snake Eyes' soldier cut into pieces, dropped like trash, scattered so everyone knew who was responsible. The block was buzzing with whispers, but Symone didn't care. She had pulled it off.

Symone slid into her black BMW coupe, her leather jacket still smelling faintly of gunpowder and cigarettes. Her braids brushed against her cheek as she tossed her bag into the passenger seat. She adjusted her mirror and smirked.

"Let that bitch Snake Eyes see this," she muttered under her breath, revving the engine.

The BMW roared down the block, tires squealing against the pavement, leaving behind a crowd of wide-eyed kids and corner boys who would be telling the story all night. Symone had a way of making even violence look like a parade.

But what she didn't see was the trap already set.

Three black SUVs had been parked in the shadows for over an hour, engines low, lights off. Snake Eyes' soldiers sat inside, weapons heavy on their laps, waiting for the signal. And a few blocks down, Snake Eyes himself sat in the backseat of a bulletproof Hummer, tinted windows hiding his cold stare. He had a cigar burning slow in his hand, his eyes fixed on the street ahead.

"This is what happens when you play with me," he muttered to himself, smoke curling around his face. "Cash wanna leave me pieces? I'll leave him broken."

Symone rolled off the block, her music blasting old school Mary J. Blige, thumping through the speakers a little too loud for her own good. She tapped the steering wheel, vibing, her mind already racing back to Cash.

But that's when she felt it.

The hairs on her arms stood up. She glanced at her mirrors. A dark SUV slid out of an alley behind her. Then another eased off a curb up ahead.

"Shit," she hissed.

Her foot pressed harder on the gas, but the street narrowed. That's when the lights flicked on. Blinding beams washed over her windshield, followed by the crack of automatic gunfire.

Bullets raked across her driver's side door. Glass shattered, spiderwebbing across the windshield. Her BMW swerved, tires screeching as she fought the wheel. Sparks lit up where bullets chewed the metal.

Symone ducked low, one hand on the wheel, the other reaching under her seat. Her Glock was waiting. She yanked it out and shouted through the chaos:

"Motherfuckers want me? COME GET ME!"

She stomped the brakes hard, the BMW jerking to a violent stop. The SUV behind her slammed the brakes too, but Symone already had her door open. She slid out low, landing hard on the pavement, returning fire.

Her shots cracked the night air, forcing one SUV to duck back. For a split second, it looked like she might carve herself a path out. But then the second SUV came roaring from the side, windows dropping. The night exploded again with gunfire.

Rounds tore into the BMW, the hood smoking, the tires shredding. And then searing pain ripped through Symone's legs. She stumbled back, blood spraying across the sidewalk.

"FUCK!" she screamed, dropping to one knee, but her Glock never wavered.

Breathing ragged, blood pouring down her jeans, Symone dragged herself to the side of the car, using it as half-cover. The night smelled of gunpowder and burning rubber, glass crunching under her palms as she pressed her back to the ruined BMW.

But she wasn't done. Not by a long shot.

"You weak-ass cowards!" she screamed across the street, her voice echoing between the brick buildings. "It take a whole fucking army to bring me down?"

Her Glock barked again. One of her bullets slammed into an SUV's headlight, glass spraying.

"You tell Snake Eyes!" she shouted, her face twisted with pain and rage. "Tell that one-eyed bitch he better finish the job himself 'cause Symone don't die easy!"

Her body was screaming for her to stop, but her spirit wouldn't let her. She leaned out again, firing until her clip ran dry. Then, hands shaking, she reloaded.

From the distance, the Hummer sat still, Snake Eyes watching it all unfold through the tinted glass. His cigar glowed in the dark, the only light on his face. His lips curled into a smile as he whispered:

"Bleed for me, girl. Show me how much you love your man."

The SUVs circled like wolves, engines growling, headlights slicing through smoke. More shooters leaned out the windows, muzzles flashing.

Bullets tore into the block. Windows shattered on bodegas, glass raining down on the pavement. Car alarms wailed. A stray bullet clipped a fire hydrant, water spraying into the street like blood from an open wound.

Symone, crouched low, fired back between gasps of pain. Her legs burned, every movement sending shocks of agony up her body. Still, she spat blood from her lip and laughed through the pain.

"This all you bitches got?!" she yelled hoarsely. "Cash gon' make y'all pay DOUBLE for this!"

She squeezed off more rounds, the Glock hot in her hand. One shooter caught a bullet to the shoulder, dropping his rifle as he slid back into the SUV screaming.

"YEAH!" Symone shouted. "Tell Snake Eyes his boys bleed just like mine!"

But then her cover gave out. The BMW's side window exploded in her face. She dove, rolling to the ground, her jeans soaking through with blood. Crawling, teeth gritted, she dragged herself toward a mailbox, trying to get another angle.

The shooters laughed cruelly, bullets pinging the ground inches from her.

"Bitch think she tough!" one of them shouted.

Symone coughed, her breath ragged, but her eyes burned with fire. "I am tough, motherfucker. Tougher than all y'all put together."

She raised the Glock again, hands trembling, and fired blind around the mailbox. The shots rang out, forcing the SUVs to pull back for just a moment.

Inside the Hummer, Snake Eyes leaned forward, resting his cigar on the ashtray. His one good eye glimmered with a predator's patience. He hadn't moved once since the first bullet fired.

"Look at her," he muttered, almost amused. "Still fighting. Still barking."

One of his lieutenants in the front seat turned. "Want me to call it off? She ain't gon' make it."

Snake Eyes shook his head slowly. "Nah. Let her bleed. Let her scream. I want Cash to hear it in her voice when she tell him what happened. Pain is louder than death."

He sipped from a glass of Hennessy, the ice clinking softly against the rim, as the war outside raged on.

Symone's vision blurred. Her Glock was almost empty again. She pressed her back to the mailbox, sweat mixing with blood dripping down her face. Somewhere in the distance, she thought she heard sirens.

Her chest rose and fell, but her mouth kept moving. "Cash… I ain't going out like this. Not tonight."

She pushed herself up, balancing on her good knee, and stepped out from behind cover, gun raised.

"COME ON, BITCHES!" she screamed. "You want Symone?! You gonna have to take me to HELL!"

Her shots rang out, wild but furious. She clipped another SUV's tire, sparks flying as the rim scraped against the pavement.

The shooters roared back in anger. All barrels turned on her.

The night turned into a storm. BRAKKA! BRAKKA! BRAKKA!

Bullets tore into the pavement, the mailbox denting under fire, the air filled with smoke and fire. One round slammed into her shoulder, spinning her to the ground. She hit the pavement hard, her Glock sliding out of reach.

Her body trembled, but her head lifted. Crawling, dragging herself forward with one arm, she reached for her gun. Her voice was hoarse, but the words carried:

"Snake Eyes… you gon' pay for this… I swear…"

She clutched the Glock again, even as blood pooled beneath her.

Far off, the sound of sirens grew louder. Blue and red lights began to flash against the buildings. Snake Eyes' men noticed first.

"Cops coming, boss!" one of the shooters yelled.

Snake Eyes smirked, leaning back in his seat. "Good. Leave the bitch breathing. That way she can tell Cash exactly who owns this city."

With a wave of his hand, the SUVs peeled off, engines roaring, gunsmoke trailing behind them. The block fell eerily quiet, broken only by the distant wail of sirens and the hiss of the fire hydrant flooding the street.

Symone lay there, trembling, her body screaming in pain. Her eyes fluttered, but she forced herself to lift her head one last time.

"Cash…" she whispered. "Don't let them… win…"

Her head fell back against the pavement as paramedics rushed in, pulling her onto a stretcher, blood soaking the white sheets. The last thing she saw before blacking out was the outline of a black Hummer at the end of the block, headlights fading into the night.

News spread fast. By the time Symone was wheeled into Harlem Hospital, word was already hitting the streets: Snake Eyes had struck back. Cash's ride-or-die was clinging to life.

The block murmured with fear, with anger, with respect. Some swore they heard her yelling through the gunfire, refusing to fold. Others said they saw her still firing after taking bullets to the legs.

And in the back room of a Harlem brownstone, Cash sat in silence when he got the call. His blunt burned down between his fingers, untouched. His jaw clenched, his knuckles white.

Snake Eyes hadn't just declared war.

He had made it personal.

Chapter 3

The hospital smelled like bleach and sickness, but Monica didn't care. She was standing against the wall, arms folded so tight her nails dug into her skin. Her eyes were locked on the red light above the double doors that read *Surgery in Progress*. That damn light had been glowing for over an hour, and every minute it stayed on, the rage inside her burned hotter.

Test was pacing in front of the vending machine, back and forth like a caged dog. His jaw kept clenching, muscles twitching in his face. Every few steps, he muttered something under his breath—curses, threats, promises he was gonna make somebody pay.

Soulja sat low in the plastic chair, hood over his head, leg bouncing like a drumbeat. He wasn't quiet because he was calm; he was quiet because his mind was calculating. Every time the sliding glass doors at the end of the hallway hissed open, his head snapped up like he was expecting enemies to come pouring through.

"Too fucking long," Test snapped, turning and throwing his fist into the vending machine so hard it rattled. "She's been in there too fucking long!"

Monica shot him a look sharp enough to cut. "You think punching that tin box is gonna speed shit up? Sit your ass down before I knock you down myself."

Test glared back, eyes bloodshot, but he didn't say nothing. He just kept pacing.

The nurse at the desk peeked up from her computer like she wanted to say something, but one look at the three of them shut her up quick. She knew what type they were. She felt the heat radiating off them and didn't want no parts.

Soulja finally spoke, voice low and steady. "If she don't make it…" He didn't even finish. He just shook his head slow, the hood shadowing his face. "If she don't make it, bodies drop. I swear to God."

Monica's lips pressed tight, then she leaned forward, elbows on her knees. "She's a soldier. Symone ain't going nowhere easy. But when she come out that room, whether she breathing or not, somebody gon' answer for it."

The silence that followed wasn't peaceful. It was thick, heavy, vibrating with fury. Every sound in the hospital—the beeps, the intercom calls, the squeak of nurses' shoes—only made the anger sharper.

Inside that operating room, Symone's world was nothing but flashing lights and muffled voices. Her body was heavy, pinned to the table, but her mind kept drifting in and out like a busted TV signal. She remembered the sparks when bullets tore into the car, the glass exploding, the heat in her legs. She remembered trying to crawl out, still spitting curses, still trying to lift her piece even when her body betrayed her.

Her chest rose and fell under the oxygen mask, every breath a battle. She heard doctors barking orders—"Clamp, now! Pressure here, she's losing blood!"—but they sounded distant, like they were shouting through water.

Symone wasn't praying. She wasn't begging. In her head, she was cussing death out. *Fuck that. You ain't taking me. Not like this. I still got shit to do. I still got heads to take off.*

The memory of Snake Eyes's Hummer flashed in her mind—the glint of his cold stare from across the street while the shots rang out. Rage shot through her chest even as her heart stuttered. She tried to move her hand, tried to ball a fist, but the anesthesia kept her locked.

Back in the waiting room, the clock ticked. Monica finally stood, unable to keep still. "I swear, when I find out who touched her, I'm burning down whole blocks. Don't care who's inside. Kids, old people, don't matter. They drew first blood."

Soulja looked up at her, and there was no argument in his eyes. "Word. Streets gon' smell like gunpowder for weeks."

Test kicked the chair in front of him so hard it skidded across the floor, crashing into the wall. The nurse flinched behind the desk, but still nobody said a word to them. Even security wasn't brave enough to check.

The doors to surgery stayed closed. That red light still burned. And with every passing second, the anger in that waiting room turned into something sharper, something violent. They weren't mourning. They were sharpening their hate like blades.

***

The hum of the warehouse lights felt like a storm ready to break. Cash stood in the middle of the floor, palms pressed down hard on the steel table. His blunt burned slow between his fingers, smoke curling around his face, but his eyes were cold fire.

Big Apple leaned back in a chair, big frame stretched out, legs wide, chewing on a toothpick like the whole world was on his nerves. He wasn't pacing, wasn't restless like Cash; he was still, the type of still that was more dangerous than movement.

"One of my guys got dropped in a fucking alley," Cash barked, slamming his fist on the table. "Like a dog, man. Like some nobody. And now Symone…" His jaw locked. He dragged hard on the blunt, exhaled smoke through his nose. "She fighting for her life while them motherfuckers breathing easy somewhere. Nah. I can't stomach that."

Big Apple finally sat up, elbows on his knees. "You acting like this a surprise. This the life, Cash. You know what comes with it. Our people get hit, their people get hit harder. That's balance. That's war."

Cash turned his glare on him. “Balance? They shot Symone up. She family. There ain’t no balance till they bleeding out the same way she bleeding right now.”

Big Apple smirked, but it wasn’t amusement—it was approval. “Good. Hold on to that. You gon’ need that fire. ’Cause from this moment forward? Ain’t no chilling. Ain’t no peace. This war don’t end till everybody who ever stood next to Snake Eyes is buried.”

The words dropped heavy, echoing in the warehouse. Cash nodded slowly, but his fists stayed tight. His mind flashed to the hospital, to Symone on that table, cut open by strangers in masks, her blood spilling while he stood here breathing. Guilt mixed with rage in his gut.

Back at the hospital, the red light still hadn’t gone off. Test was pacing so hard it looked like he’d wear a groove in the tile. Monica had her phone out, checking for updates from Cash, but she kept locking the screen and muttering, “Hurry the fuck up.”

Soulja’s voice cut through. “Y’all feel that?”

Monica frowned. “Feel what?”

“Air thick,” Soulja said. He sat up straighter, eyes sharp now. “It’s too quiet in here. Too damn quiet. Like they know we here.”

Test pulled his hoodie tighter, hand brushing the piece tucked in his waistband. “If anybody dumb enough to walk through them doors with Snake Eyes on they chest, I’ma drop ‘em right here in the ER.”

Monica’s lips curled into a snarl. “Word. Let ‘em try. They gon’ carry two bodies outta here tonight.”

Still, nobody came. No enemies, no nurses with answers—just the same clock ticking, ticking, ticking, winding their nerves tighter with every second.

Inside the operating room, Symone’s heartbeat stuttered on the monitor. The doctor’s voice rose. “Pressure’s dropping. Get me more units, now!” The team moved like lightning. Symone drifted deeper, but her mind clawed against the dark.

In her head, she was back on the block, gun in her hand, yelling, "I ain't going nowhere till every last one of y'all is dead!" Her vision swam with flashes of Snake Eyes's grin, the muzzle flash of rifles, the taste of blood in her mouth. She wanted out that bed. She wanted back on the street.

Her heart kicked back into rhythm like her rage dragged her soul from the edge. The doctor didn't know what pushed her body to keep fighting, but Symone did. It was hate. Pure, burning hate.

At the warehouse, Cash snatched up his phone. He stared at the screen like he could will it to ring. Big Apple watched him, voice calm but sharp.

"You keep checking that phone like it's gon' change something. She either makes it or she don't. But while you sitting here waiting, Snake Eyes breathing. Snake Eyes plotting. You gon' wait till he hit again, or you gon' hit first?"

Cash ground his teeth. "We hitting tonight."

Big Apple's eyes lit up with something cold. "Now you talking my language."

Cash's mind snapped back to Symone. He pictured her strapped to tubes, her body full of holes, still fighting. If she could fight, so could he. And the only way to honor that fight was to spill blood.

Back in the hospital, the red light above the surgery doors finally went dark. The double doors creaked open, and a surgeon stepped out, mask pulled down, eyes tired.

Monica, Test, and Soulja shot to their feet, closing in like wolves.

"How she doing?" Monica demanded, voice sharp enough to cut.

The doctor hesitated a split second too long, and Test snapped, grabbing him by the collar. "Spit it the fuck out!"

"She's alive," the doctor said quickly, words tumbling out. "But she lost a lot of blood. We stabilized her, but the next twenty-four hours are critical. She'll be in recovery soon, but it's still a very touch-and-go situation. No promises that she's making it, but we have her stable right now."

That was all Monica needed. She turned to Test and Soulja, jaw clenched. "She's alive. That's enough."

Test let the doctor go with a shove, stepping back, chest still heaving.

Soulja nodded slow, his hood falling back enough to show the fire in his eyes. "Then we don't waste time. Cash need to know she breathing so he can start the war. Tonight."

Monica's voice was low, dangerous. "Tonight. We tear the city apart. Every alley, every corner—Snake Eyes gon' wish he never crossed us."

The rage in that waiting room wasn't just heat anymore. It was solid. It was focus. And it was about to flood the streets.

***

The engines growled like predators, low and dangerous, cutting through the midnight air. Blacked-out SUVs and muscle cars rolled slow down the avenues, tires skimming the wet asphalt, smoke curling from the tailpipes. Inside the front car, Cash's hands gripped the steering wheel so tight his knuckles shined white in the dim interior lights. Big Apple sat in the passenger seat, calm and collected, eyes scanning the streets like a hawk, while Test and Soulja rode in the rear with a dozen shooters, each one loaded and ready to strike.

Monica sat off to the side, perched on the hood of a beat-up Escalade, map in hand. Her eyes were sharp, tracking locations and whispering coordinates to the crew through a cracked earpiece. "Trap house on Third and Davis. Auto shop on Elm. Corner store on 7th. Everybody go heavy. Block all exits. No mercy," she barked, her voice carrying authority that cut through the roar of engines.

Cash exhaled smoke from the blunt dangling off his lips. "Tonight we make a statement. Snake Eyes' whole fucking operation gets fucked. His boys bleed, his cash gone, his corners ours. Let's move."

The convoy shifted forward like a pack of wolves, rolling past dim streetlights and flickering neon lights.

The first stop was the auto parts shop on Elm. Cash's shooters hit the lot like ghosts. Tires screeched, glass shattered, and men ran screaming. Cash moved with precision, his eyes locked on anyone making a move. Test and Soulja had positions covering all exits.

"Front and back!" Monica's voice hissed in their earpieces. "Roof line covered! Don't let nobody slip!"

The shooters did their work clean. Guns sprayed through windows, bodies crumpled to the floor, and the crew stripped the place of cash, guns, and anything of value. Cash's own rifle barked twice, taking out one of Snake Eyes' men trying to escape through the back alley.

Big Apple moved silent like a shadow, flipping tables and shattering cash registers with his boots. "Nothing left for them to use," he said coldly, stepping over a body as if it were nothing.

By the time the crew pulled back into the street, the first auto shop had been cleared. Cash's convoy moved like a storm, leaving nothing but destruction behind.

The city had no chance to catch its breath. Muscle cars and SUVs rolled slow along Main Street. The shooters leaned out of windows, automatic weapons rattling off, tearing through Snake Eyes' crew who had been waiting in the shadows to retaliate. Tires popped under gunfire, glass sprayed across the asphalt, and screams echoed off the brick walls.

Test's voice cut through the chaos. "Left side, alley three! Cut off their escape!"

Soulja's car slid to a stop at the intersection, shooters disembarking and pushing forward into the cross streets.

Bullets sprayed everywhere. A man ran from a corner store only to get cut off by a shooter, pinned against a wall. The crew moved like a single unit—precise, violent, unstoppable.

Big Apple's sniper rifle cracked over the rooftops, picking off targets attempting to flee. Cash waved his hand, signaling the shooters to push further into Snake Eyes' territory. They moved with military precision: trap houses, auto shops, and corners all systematically hit.

Even as the streets burned, Monica kept one eye on her phone. Symone's monitors flashed on the hospital screen, her heartbeat steady but fragile. Every hit, every stolen stash, every bullet fired—it was for her. She hadn't fired a shot, but she was orchestrating the chaos like a master general.

Monica barked coordinates. "Next trap house, 9th and Vine. Push hard. Don't give them time to regroup."

Inside the hospital, Symone drifted in and out of consciousness. The sound of her own labored breathing mixed with the faint echo of gunfire in her mind. Even unconscious, her survival fueled the crew's rage. Each flashback of bullets ripping through her car played like a drumbeat, pushing them to move faster, hit harder, kill more efficiently.

Snake Eyes' men were scrambling now. They weren't expecting such coordination. Every alley had shooters. Every corner had eyes. Cars roamed like predators, tires smoking, engines growling. The streets were a warzone.

In the first trap house, Cash's shooters executed clean kills while taking cash and guns. Big Apple cleared another, moving like death incarnate, leaving bodies where they fell. Test and Soulja handled perimeter suppression, ensuring no one escaped.

Cars screeched down side streets, bullets ricocheted, and explosions rocked abandoned lots. Flames licked at trash cans, tires, and the cracked asphalt. Civilians fled, ducking into doorways, covering their heads. This wasn't chaos. This was strategy executed with maximum violence.

Monica's voice cut through their earpieces again, precise and cold. "Trap house on 12th. Corner blocked. Push fast. Leave nothing."

Cash and Big Apple coordinated a strike on Snake Eyes' lieutenant holed up in a garage full of stolen auto parts. The doors burst open; gunfire tore through the air. Cash dove behind a stack of tires, returning fire with measured rage. The lieutenant went down with a guttural scream, blood painting the concrete.

Outside, Big Apple's shooters had hit multiple trap houses at the same time. Test and Soulja cornered fleeing targets, their rifles cutting through any attempt at escape. Cash moved from car to car, directing shooters, wiping sweat from his brow, eyes burning red.

Monica watched from a safe position, calculating the next moves, marking cleared zones, and assigning shooters to mop up. Every stolen stash, every corpse, every piece of territory taken—they all added to the pile of Snake Eyes' crumbling empire.

By dawn, the streets were quiet. Bodies littered corners and trap houses, the air thick with gunpowder and smoke. Tire marks and broken glass shone wet under the first light. Cars were gone, looted, abandoned. Cash, Big Apple, Test, and Soulja regrouped in the lot, engines still idling, weapons slick with blood and oil.

Monica counted loot, updated the map, her eyes sharp. Not a shot fired by her, yet she had directed the chaos that left Snake Eyes' empire bleeding.

Cash wiped sweat from his brow, his grin cold, hard. "This ain't the end," he said, voice low. "This is just act one. We go bigger next time. Snake Eyes gonna wish he never showed his face."

The crew nodded in agreement, silent, heavy with anticipation. They knew the streets belonged to them for now, but the war had only begun.

Chapter 4

The room was thick with heat, music low and pulsing like a heartbeat, the kind that wraps around your skin and makes the air itself feel alive. Red Invee's laugh was soft, teasing, as Snake Eyes' hands traced her curves, memorizing every inch of her in the dim, golden glow of the lamp. His lips found hers again and again, tasting, claiming, lost in a rhythm that belonged only to them.

"Snake," she murmured, voice sultry, her fingers threading through his hair, pulling him closer. The world outside their small sanctuary didn't exist. It was just them—the music, the skin, the sweat, the hungry glances, and half-smiles that said more than words ever could.

He pressed her against him, feeling the warmth of her body, letting the tension between them build. Everything about Red Invee drew him in: the sway of her hips, the fire in her eyes, the way her lips curved when she was teasing him. For a brief, perfect moment, nothing mattered but the heat, the passion, the closeness of the woman in his arms.

And then the phone buzzed.

Snake Eyes froze, a groan escaping his throat, a hand reluctantly breaking the connection between them to snatch up the device. "What?" His voice was low, but every muscle in his body tensed, the intimacy vanishing in an instant.

"Snake… it's bad," came the tense, urgent voice of his second-in-command. "Your guys—they got hit. Robbed. Killed. On the block. Cash's men. It's chaos out here."

The words hit him like a hammer. The world tilted, the heat, the passion—everything in that room—shattering in a single, brutal instant. He shoved Red Invee away, more roughly than he intended, the sudden loss of contact leaving both of them gasping.

"Snake, what's wrong?" she asked, fear and confusion coloring her voice as she sat back on the bed, her hair falling around her shoulders like a curtain.

He didn't answer, didn't speak; his jaw clenched, eyes dark with something fierce and unstoppable. The phone crackled again, pouring more of the nightmare into his ears. Images of his men lying dead, operations gutted, his turf violated—the chaos hitting him in waves, each one sharper than the last.

Red Invee reached toward him, but he recoiled instinctively. "Don't," he growled, voice low, dangerous. The intimacy, the closeness—they were gone. Replaced by a predator, a man whose world had been ripped apart in seconds.

He slammed the phone onto the nightstand, fists tightening, veins standing out on his forearms. Rage radiated off him in waves so strong it seemed to make the walls shake. Red Invee's eyes widened, and she swallowed hard, realizing she had just been thrust out of a world she could no longer touch.

Snake Eyes' breathing was heavy, deliberate—controlled yet explosive. Every part of him screamed for retaliation, for blood, for fire. The soft warmth that had been between them moments ago was gone, replaced by the ice-cold certainty that the streets would burn before this went unanswered.

"Red… get out of here," he said finally, voice clipped, sharp as broken glass. "Now."

She hesitated, hand lingering toward him, but the storm in his eyes—the raw anger—left no room for argument. Slowly, reluctantly, she stepped back, sensing the war that had just awakened in the man she knew, feeling it in the air like static before a lightning strike.

Snake Eyes picked up the phone again, dialing another number with shaking hands, eyes blazing with fury. Every muscle in his body was coiled, every thought sharpened, every plan for vengeance forming in an instant. Cash had crossed him, and the streets would feel the full force of what it meant to wake a man like Snake Eyes.

Red Invee watched him, her heart pounding not with passion now, but with fear and awe. She had seen the fire in him before, but nothing like this. In the span of moments, he had shifted from desire to wrath, from lover to predator, and she realized he would let nothing, no one, stand in his way.

The music still played low, but it was meaningless now, drowned out by the storm that had taken over the room. Snake Eyes didn't glance back at her, didn't touch her, didn't speak beyond terse commands into the phone. The man she had just been wrapped in, the one whose lips and hands had set her skin on fire, had vanished, replaced by the cold fury of a warlord whose territory and his men had been violated.

And in that moment, Red Invee understood something crucial: passion could wait. Vengeance could not.

***

The fluorescent lights of the hospital corridor buzzed faintly overhead, cold and unwelcoming. Detectives Harris and Molina moved down the hall with quiet, purposeful steps, their shoes clicking against the polished floor. The air smelled of antiseptic and burnt coffee, reminders that this place ran on both medicine and exhaustion.

ICU was a different world inside the hospital. Behind the double doors, silence pressed down heavy, broken only by the steady hum of machines and the occasional beeping from a monitor. Nurses moved like shadows, quick but calm, as though every second mattered.

They stopped outside Room 214. Symone lay there, half-hidden beneath a tangle of tubes and wires. Her face was pale, lips cracked, and a faint line of dried blood still clung to her hairline. Her chest rose and fell slowly with the rhythm of the ventilator, a machine doing the work her body couldn't.

Detective Harris glanced through the glass, jaw tightening. "She's tougher than she looks," he muttered, voice low.

Molina folded his arms. "She's lucky to even be breathing. You seen what they did to that car? Looked like it went through a war zone."

A doctor in a white coat approached, clipboard in hand, eyes tired behind his glasses. He slowed when he saw the detectives, reading the weight on their faces before speaking.

"You're here for Symone Carter," the doctor said flatly.

"That's right," Harris answered, stepping forward. "How is she?"

The doctor let out a slow breath. "She took multiple gunshot wounds to the legs and lower abdomen. Lost a lot of blood before the paramedics got her stabilized. Right now, she's in critical condition, sedated, and on heavy medication. We've repaired what we could, but…" He hesitated, searching for the right word. "It's touch and go."

Molina leaned in, his tone sharp. "You saying she might not make it?"

The doctor adjusted his glasses, unflinching. "I'm saying she's alive because she fought hard. But her body is fragile. If there's any more complications—bleeding, infection—it could go either way."

The silence that followed was thick, broken only by the faint beep from Symone's monitor. Harris glanced at her through the glass again. She looked so still it was hard to imagine the fire she was known for, the woman who never backed down, who spit curses at gunmen even as bullets tore into her.

"She conscious at all?" Harris asked.

"Not fully," the doctor said. "We've kept her under to manage the pain and keep her stable. If she wakes, it'll be brief, and she won't be in any condition to talk."

Molina cursed under his breath, running a hand across his jaw. "Damn. She's the only one who could tell us what went down. The streets are locked tight; no one's talking. She might be the key."

Harris stayed quiet, eyes fixed on Symone. He wasn't just thinking about the case. He was thinking about the war spilling across the city—Snake Eyes, Cash, Big Apple. Every night, more bodies dropped, and here was another soldier caught in the storm.

The doctor shifted his weight, lowering his voice. "Look, I know you want answers. But right now, the best thing you can do is let her rest. If she pulls through, you'll get your chance. If not…" He let the sentence hang in the sterile air.

Harris nodded stiffly. "We'll wait."

The detectives turned, stepping back from the glass. Symone lay unmoving, but in that silence, in the mechanical rhythm of her breathing machine, there was a fragile defiance. She wasn't gone yet.

And if she woke, she would have plenty to say.

***

The bass of the club thumped low, a rhythm that seemed to match the heartbeat of the city outside. Smoke curled lazily toward the ceiling, catching the dim colored lights and giving the room a haze that made everything feel unreal, almost dreamlike. Snake Eyes sat behind a small velvet rope near the back, a glass of dark liquor in hand, watching his club like a king surveying his kingdom. His soldiers, lean and quiet, leaned against walls and tables, eyes scanning every doorway. The place was mostly empty tonight, save for the familiar faces he trusted.

The click of heels against the polished floor pulled Snake Eyes' attention toward the entrance. Two detectives stepped in, badges tucked under their jackets, hands empty, but their presence demanding space. Harris and Molina were no strangers to the streets, but stepping into one of Snake Eyes' clubs was different. Here, the air smelled of danger, not perfume or alcohol.

Snake Eyes lifted a brow but didn't rise. The detectives walked confidently toward him, though their eyes flicked to the men lining the room. Harris cleared his throat first.

"Snake Eyes," he said, voice low but firm. "We need to talk."

Snake Eyes leaned back, letting his gaze travel over them slowly, like a predator assessing the next move of prey. He said nothing at first, just sipped his drink, savoring the tension.

Molina spoke next. "Look, we're rooting for you. You know we're not blind to what's going on. Cash is moving fast, leaving bodies behind. You're slipping."

The words hit the room like a cold gust. Snake Eyes didn't flinch, but inside, the irritation rose like heat behind his eyes. *Sloppy? Me?* He thought. *Let them think that. Let them see the storm coming.*

"You think I don't know what I'm doing?" Snake Eyes finally said, voice smooth, dangerous. "Bodies dropping? That's the game, detective. You think I sit here and watch while the world moves without me?"

Harris shook his head, leaning in slightly. "No, we get that. But this isn't the time for pride. The streets are talking. Cash is winning right now, Snake Eyes. If you don't tighten up, you're losing."

Snake Eyes studied him for a long moment, lips pressed into a thin line. *Winning? The streets don't decide who wins; I do.*

"And what do you want from me?" Snake Eyes asked finally, calm as ever, though his eyes gleamed with something colder.

"Just… don't make it worse," Molina said. "We know you're capable. But if this war keeps going like this, more bodies are gonna fall, and not just theirs. Yours too."

Snake Eyes smiled faintly, a predator's smile, not friendly. "I appreciate the concern. But the streets? They'll learn respect the hard way. And if that's not enough… they'll learn the easy way. Now, you two… you should leave before you get caught in the crossfire."

The detectives nodded, knowing better than to argue further. They turned to leave, eyes scanning every shadow as Snake Eyes' gaze followed them, cold and calculating. Once the door closed, he leaned back fully, his mind already moving faster than theirs could imagine.

The night had just begun, and Snake Eyes wasn't one to wait. He gathered his men in the backroom, the smell of gun oil and stale smoke heavy in the air. Every face he saw was loyal, sharp, ready. He laid out the plan like a master strategist: drive-bys on Cash's key operations, quick hits to his soldiers, a message that would bleed through the city by morning.

"Tonight, they learn," he said, voice low, almost a growl. "No hesitation. No mercy. Watch the streets light up like they never have before. Cash thinks he's winning? Let's show him what losing feels like."

By midnight, Snake Eyes' crew was moving, slipping through dark alleys and empty streets, guns loaded, hearts steady. The city seemed unaware, asleep under the yellow streetlights, but soon it would wake to chaos.

The first block was quiet. Cash's men weren't expecting this. The shooters fanned out, silent shadows in black hoodies. Snake Eyes watched from a nearby alley, perched like a hawk, eyes tracking every movement. A car pulled up, three of Cash's lieutenants stepping out, laughing too loud in the night.

Then it began.

Bullets ripped through the air, shattering glass, striking flesh, sending men to the ground before they could react. The sound of gunfire echoed down the streets, terrifying and precise. Snake Eyes' men moved like shadows, deadly and coordinated, each shot a sentence, each body a message.

By the end of the first wave, the streets were a scene of chaos—cars sprayed with bullets, blood marking the asphalt, Cash's soldiers scrambling in shock and terror. Snake Eyes sat in his club calmly, calculating the next move, his own pulse steady while chaos tore through the city like a storm he had called.

He didn't celebrate, didn't yell. That wasn't his way. Instead, he lit a cigarette, smoke curling around him like a halo, and observed the aftermath. The message was clear: Snake Eyes didn't miss. Snake Eyes didn't hesitate. Snake Eyes was patient, and deadly.

By the time the sun began to rise, the first news reports hit: multiple casualties on Cash's side, unidentified shooters, city streets screaming the aftermath. Snake Eyes retreated to his club, slipping inside unnoticed, blending back into the smoke and shadows.

Inside, the club was quiet, the bass now just a hum. His men returned, reporting clean hits, casualties confirmed, the map of their strike spread out before him. Snake Eyes sat, calm as ever, eyes scanning, planning the next move.

The war had only just escalated. Bodies were dropping. Messages sent. The city already knew: Snake Eyes was here, and he was just getting started.

Chapter 5

The smell of acetone and nail polish filled the little salon on the corner of Fulton and Troy. Snake Eyes' wife, Alana, leaned back in her chair as the nail tech shaped her hands with slow, careful strokes. Outside, Brooklyn moved at its usual restless pace—buses roaring by, kids laughing too loud, and the constant thump of bass from passing cars.

She smiled faintly, enjoying the rare calm. Life with Snake Eyes was never quiet, never soft, but here, for a brief hour, she could pretend she was just another woman getting her nails done. Her bodyguard, Derrick, sat by the door in a black hoodie, eyes scanning everything with the kind of focus only years in the streets could carve into a man.

Alana checked her phone—no new messages. Relief. Because lately, Snake Eyes' enemies had been moving differently. Cash's crew, Big Apple's dogs—everybody wanted blood. She knew she wasn't untouchable, but she trusted Derrick. That was Snake Eyes' best soldier, the one man he trusted to move her around without hesitation.

Then the glass door pushed open. A little bell jingled.

Alana didn't look up right away. But Derrick did. His hand slid toward the inside of his hoodie, where the handle of his Glock rested.

Three men walked in. Not customers. Not friendly.

At the front was Big Apple—broad shoulders, thick neck, eyes that stayed cold no matter what room he walked into. His presence alone froze the air. Behind him were two shadows: Slim, tall and wiry, his face twisted in a smirk, and Momo, heavier, eyes dead like he'd lost his soul years ago.

The salon went silent. The nail tech froze mid-brush.

Derrick stood. "Ayo, this ain't the spot," he said, voice tight. "Back out the door."

Big Apple grinned without humor. "Relax, lil' homie. We just here for a conversation." His voice was gravel, calm in a way that meant danger.

Alana's stomach dropped. She knew that voice. She had heard Snake Eyes curse his name more times than she could count.

Derrick moved first, hand pulling the Glock. He didn't hesitate, but he didn't get the chance.

Slim was faster than he looked, swinging a pistol from under his coat and firing once. The crack of the shot shook the salon. Derrick's body jolted, the bullet slamming into his chest. He stumbled back into the wall, gasping as blood spread across his hoodie.

Alana screamed.

Big Apple didn't flinch. He just stepped forward, pointing at her with one thick finger. "Get up."

The nail tech scrambled out of the way, running toward the back door. Nobody cared.

Alana froze, her mind screaming for her body to move. "Please, please, don't—"

Momo came around and yanked her by the arm, pulling her up from the chair so hard her wrist cracked. She tried to fight him, scratching, clawing, but he slammed her against the wall.

"Shut her up," Big Apple ordered.

Slim ripped a strip of duct tape from his jacket pocket and slapped it across her mouth. She cried out beneath it, muffled, tears already streaking her face.

Derrick coughed, sliding down the wall, trying to lift his gun. Big Apple stepped over and stomped down hard on Derrick's wrist, the bones snapping with a sick crunch. Derrick groaned, the weapon clattering uselessly to the floor.

"You shoulda stayed out the way," Big Apple said, raising his own .44 Magnum. He aimed without hesitation and pulled the trigger. The blast thundered through the room, Derrick's head snapping back as blood sprayed across the pale wall.

Alana's legs gave out beneath her, but Momo held her up like dead weight.

Big Apple turned, face hard as stone. "Put her in the van."

The two soldiers dragged her out, ignoring the terrified gasps of the women huddled at the back of the salon. Nobody was brave enough to follow. Nobody was calling the cops. Not here. Not with Big Apple's name tied to it.

Outside, the late afternoon sun painted the street in gold. A black van waited by the curb, engine already running. They shoved her inside, slammed the door, and the world shrank to metal walls, stale cigarette smoke, and fear so thick she could taste it.

Big Apple sat across from her as the van sped off. The .44 rested in his lap, polished steel catching the light. He leaned forward, studying her like she was nothing more than a problem to be solved.

"You know why this is happening, don't you?" he asked.

Her eyes were wide, tears spilling, head shaking desperately. The tape muffled her cries, but her terror filled the space louder than words.

Big Apple smirked. "Your husband think he untouchable. Think he can move sloppy, think he can talk slick about Apple like I'm just another corner boy. Nah. He forgot. I built this block before he even knew how to hold a pistol. And now?" He tapped the gun lightly against his palm. "Now he gon' learn what it means to cross me."

Slim chuckled low, glancing back from the front passenger seat. "She look like she already know, boss. Look at her shaking like a leaf."

Momo said nothing, just stared at her with those dead eyes, like he was already digging her grave in his mind.

Alana tried to speak, tried to beg, but the tape turned her voice into broken sobs. She thought of Snake Eyes, of the last kiss they shared before she left the house, of his laugh, his hands, his promise that nothing would ever touch her. That promise shattered now, burning in her chest like betrayal.

Big Apple leaned closer until his face was inches from hers. “Don’t worry. He gon’ see you again. On my terms.”

He pulled out his phone and started setting up the camera.

The van drove deeper into Brooklyn, leaving behind the noise of Fulton for the quiet of abandoned warehouses and empty lots. They stopped near an overgrown field—weeds tall, fences rusted, no witnesses for blocks.

The door slid open, and Momo dragged her out into the dirt. She stumbled, the tape still across her mouth, wrists bound behind her with zip ties. Her knees hit the ground hard, skin scraping raw.

Big Apple stepped out slowly, rolling his shoulders, savoring the moment. “This the part where Snake Eyes gon’ understand what I mean when I say I don’t play.”

He looked down at her, tilting his head like she was less than human. Then he aimed the .44 at her trembling body, pausing just long enough for Slim to set the camera phone up steady.

“Make sure you get everything,” Big Apple said.

Slim nodded. “We live, boss.”

The camera’s red light blinked steady, catching the evening glow as it settled on Alana’s tear-streaked face. Her chest heaved, every breath shallow and desperate, muffled sobs breaking through the strip of tape.

Big Apple crouched beside her, the massive .44 glinting in his hand. His voice was calm, almost conversational, but every word dripped venom.

“You see, Snake Eyes…” He looked straight into the lens now, speaking as if his rival was already watching. “This what happens when you forget who run these streets. You think you the king. You think Cash is your only problem. Nah, boy. It's me. And I just showed you."

He grabbed a handful of Alana's hair, yanking her head back so her face filled the frame. She whimpered through the tape, eyes pleading.

"She ain't deserve this," Big Apple went on, tone cruel but steady. "But this blood? It's on your hands. Every tear, every scream she makin'… that's your fault. Remember that."

He pressed the barrel of the Magnum to her temple. She thrashed, muffled screams turning frantic, body shaking like it might split apart. Slim kept the camera steady, zooming in on the steel against her skin.

"World gon' see this," Slim muttered, half in awe, half in fear.

"No," Big Apple corrected, eyes never leaving the lens. "Only Snake Eyes. He the one I want broken."

Without hesitation, he squeezed the trigger.

The sound ripped through the field, echoing off the broken fences and hollow warehouses. Alana's body went limp instantly, crumpling into the dirt as blood bloomed beneath her.

Slim lowered the phone, exhaling. Even Momo blinked, though his face stayed stone.

Big Apple stood, towering over the lifeless body. For a moment, silence pressed down heavy. Then he turned to his men. "Grab that mutt."

Momo walked to the back of the van. From a thick tarp, he pulled out the carcass of a dead pit bull, stiff and reeking. They had picked it up earlier from a back alley, part of Apple's twisted plan.

"Dig," Big Apple ordered.

They took shovels from the van and started tearing into the earth. The ground was hard, but adrenaline made the work quick. Dirt flew, piling up as the hole widened. Six feet deep, Big Apple signaled for them to stop.

"Drop it."

Alana hit the bottom with a sick thud. Her body twisted awkwardly in the dirt. Slim gagged faintly at the look of her.

Big Apple looked down, satisfied. "Get ready to drop the dog down. That's insurance. Cops ever come sniffin' with their dogs, they gon' stop right there."

They started throwing dirt over her body until they were four feet deep. Sweat dripped down their faces, the city's night noises creeping in—the distant rumble of a train, a dog barking far away, the whisper of wind through weeds.

When it was done, Big Apple nodded toward the dead dog. "Put it in."

Momo and Slim lifted the dog, laying it gently on top of the dirt. The sight was grotesque—the wife of one of Brooklyn's most feared men, reduced to a hidden grave with a mutt as her bedfellow.

Big Apple crouched again, staring at the hole with two lifeless bodies one last time. "Snake Eyes gon' dig through hell lookin' for you. And he ain't never gon' find nothin' but a dog."

He spat into the dirt, then motioned for them to cover it.

Shovel after shovel, the earth swallowed her. Soon the grave was level, just another patch of dirt in a forgotten field. Big Apple stamped it down with his boot, erasing the last sign of what had happened.

"Record this too," he told Slim.

Slim lifted the phone again as Big Apple looked straight into the lens. His voice came low, like thunder ready to break.

"Snake Eyes, you wanted war. Well, now you got it. And I promise you, by the time I'm done, you gon' beg me for mercy."

He smirked, then cut the recording.

Later that night, Snake Eyes sat in his study, a half-burned cigar resting in an ashtray, a glass of Hennessy untouched at his side. His phone buzzed.

Unknown number.

He frowned, picking it up. One video file. No text. No explanation. Just the file.

Something in his chest turned cold. He hit play.

The screen filled with Big Apple's face, grinning like the devil himself. Then it shifted—Alana, bound, terrified, eyes begging for help that would never come. Snake Eyes' breath caught, his knuckles whitening around the phone.

The gun appeared. The words followed. Snake Eyes couldn't even hear them anymore; his pulse pounded too loud, rage boiling in his skull. But he saw it. He saw the barrel press to her head. He saw her flinch. He saw her die.

The phone slipped from his hand, clattering onto the desk. His chest heaved, his whole body trembling, but not from grief—no tears came. Only fire.

Every vein in his body screamed for blood.

Snake Eyes stood, fists clenched, his voice breaking the silence of the room.

"Big Apple…" He whispered it once, then louder, then roared it like thunder shaking the walls. "Big Apple!"

He kicked the desk over, the glass of Hennessy shattering against the floor, cigar rolling into the corner. His men came running, but one look at their boss told them everything. His eyes were pure murder.

"Round everybody up," Snake Eyes snarled. "I don't care where they at. Tonight, we move. Tonight, Apple gon' learn who he just declared war on."

Big Apple, back in his hideout, poured himself a drink, the video already sent, the game already in motion. He knew Snake Eyes would come for him. He wanted it that way.

Because Big Apple wasn't just trying to kill Snake Eyes.

He wanted to break him first.

***

Cash stepped into the room, the news of his LTs' deaths still fresh in his mind, but instead of rage, a cold, calculated focus began to settle over him. His heart thumped with a controlled intensity, not chaos. He clenched his fists, feeling the weight of loss, but it was already sharpening his mind, not dulling it.

The door opened quietly. Big Apple stepped in, the unmistakable scent of a lit blunt trailing behind him. Smoke curled lazily around him as he leaned against the doorframe, eyes on Cash. There was no rush, no panic in his posture—just the calm of a man who knew the chaos he'd just set in motion.

"I just sent Snake Eyes a real fucking message," Big Apple said smoothly, the blunt dangling between his fingers. "One that's gonna hit him where it hurts the most."

Cash raised an eyebrow, a slight smirk tugging at the corner of his mouth. "Oh? That so?" he said, stepping closer, intrigued. The weight of what Big Apple had done wasn't lost on him. There was an artistry in cruelty when executed with precision.

Big Apple took a slow drag, letting the smoke drift between them, then exhaled. "Wanna see it?" He pulled out his phone and held it out, almost lazily.

Cash nodded, a glint in his eye. "Let's see how he handles it." He didn't sound angry; he sounded approving. Dangerous approval, but approval nonetheless.

Big Apple tapped a few buttons, and the screen lit up. There she was—Cash's LT's wife—the video raw and brutal, recorded just before her death. Cash's eyes didn't flare with rage. Instead, they narrowed, focused, impressed by the cold precision of the message. Every detail, every moment, calculated to break Snake Eyes emotionally.

"Damn…" Cash muttered, almost to himself, shaking his head slightly. "That's… impressive. You didn't just kill her; you made him watch. You made him feel it in his chest."

Big Apple leaned back, a faint smirk beneath the smoke curling from his lips. “Exactly. I wanted him to understand, not just see.”

Cash reached for a bottle on the counter, twisting the cap thoughtfully but not opening it. He exhaled slowly, letting the tension in his shoulders ease just slightly. Then he picked up the blunt Big Apple had been smoking and took a long drag himself, passing it back with a nod of approval.

“Fuck her dead body,” Cash said, voice low and deliberate. “Let him feel every second. Let him know what losing someone looks like. Make him question every move he’s made, every street he’s stepped on.”

Big Apple’s eyes glinted, sensing the alignment of their minds. “That’s the plan,” he said, tapping the screen. “And when he sees it, he’s going to crumble.”

Cash leaned against the counter, eyes on the phone, not with anger, but with admiration. “You handled that perfectly. No mess, no chaos—just the message. The art of it.” He shook his head, smirk widening. “Damn, I gotta hand it to you… this one’s gonna sting.”

Big Apple chuckled softly, smoke curling around his face. “I told you, Cash. Sometimes the deadliest moves aren’t the ones that make noise; they’re the ones that echo in someone’s head long after it’s over.”

Cash took another drag of the blunt, letting it calm him, sharpen him at the same time. “Yeah… echo. That’s exactly what he’s gonna get. He won’t know what hit him until it’s too late. Send it to me now.”

Big Apple nodded and tapped the phone, sending the video directly to Cash. Cash didn’t flinch, didn’t tense; he merely watched, a predator pleased with a well-laid trap. The loss of his LTs had shifted into fuel, and now the fire was cold, calculated, and merciless.

“Perfect,” Cash murmured, exhaling smoke slowly. “Let’s see how he handles that.” He dropped the phone back onto the counter and grinned, dark and confident. "Snake Eyes isn't ready for this."

The room was quiet, the only sound the soft hum of the city outside and the faint crackle of the blunt. Inside, two men, aligned and dangerous, were already setting the pieces for the next move. And when the storm hit, it would leave nothing standing in its wake.

***

Snake Eyes stared at the phone screen, his grip so tight the device threatened to shatter in his hands. The video played again, over and over, like a twisted loop designed to burn into his soul. He didn't hear the faint buzzing of the city outside, didn't notice the hum of his car engine in the dark garage. All he saw was her—her terrified eyes, the raw panic in her voice, and then the final, unthinkable act.

He dropped the phone onto the concrete floor. It bounced once, then skidded to a stop, but he didn't care. He didn't need it in his hands to feel the impact. Rage, hotter than fire, rolled through him, making his limbs rigid, his chest heave, his vision narrow. He wanted to scream, to break something—anything—but the sound never came. Instead, he clenched his fists until his nails dug into his palms.

Hate blossomed in his chest, cold and consuming. Not the kind of hate that fades. This was a hatred sharpened by helplessness, a precise, surgical kind of fury that demanded retribution. Every second that ticked by without her in the world was a second he swore would be repaid in blood.

He replayed the video again, each frame engraving itself deeper into his mind. He memorized the shooter's stance, the surroundings, the cadence of the gunshot. Not for shock. Not for grief. For war.

Snake Eyes didn't cry. He didn't collapse. He stood in the shadows of his garage, the glow from the phone painting his face in ghostly light, and made a vow. Big Apple would feel this. Every one of his men, every resource, every corner of the streets he controlled—they would all be turned against the man who dared to take her from him.

He whispered her name once, low, lethal, and carried it out into the empty garage like a threat to the universe itself. Then he bent down, picked up the phone, and with a chilling calmness, said aloud to himself, "They're going to pay. Every last one of them."

Cold fury replaced despair. Hatred replaced helplessness. And Snake Eyes, silent and deadly, began plotting the destruction of anyone responsible for the life they stole.

***

Detective Cross sat alone in the dimly lit bar, his phone propped against his glass of whiskey. On the screen, photos of his family stared back at him—smiles frozen in time, laughter captured in pixels, reminders of everything Big Apple had tried to take from him. His jaw tightened as he scrolled slowly, each picture stabbing him with a mix of love and grief. He touched one image of his daughter laughing in the sun, then another of his wife smiling, and the fury in his chest flared hotter.

He didn't notice the bar's chatter anymore, or the low hum of music. He was somewhere else, replaying every loss, every betrayal, every death. His hand gripped the edge of the table so tightly his knuckles went white.

Then someone bumped his chair lightly, unthinkingly, as they passed by.

Cross's head snapped up, eyes blazing like coals. "Watch it," he growled, voice low but sharp enough to cut through the bar's noise.

The person, a young man with an apologetic grin, stepped back. "Sorry, man, didn't see you there."

"Didn't see me?" Cross repeated, his tone now a dangerous purr. "I don't get bumped. Not tonight."

In a flash, he lunged, grabbing the man by the collar and slamming him against the bar. Glasses rattled, patrons shouted, and the man tried to explain himself, but Cross wasn't listening. Rage—personal, unchecked—coursed through him. He struck again and again, each blow sharper, harder, fueled by the memories of his family, by the sight of their photos moments ago.

By the time the bartender yelled at him to stop, the man was on the floor, clutching his face, groaning in pain, frantically reaching for his phone. Cross's chest heaved, eyes dark with a storm of grief and fury. The man fumbled, dialing the cops, panic in his voice, but Cross didn't move. He simply stood, looming over the chaos he'd created, breathing hard, like a predator savoring the control.

The bar had gone silent, all eyes on him, some in fear, others in disbelief. Cross looked down at the battered man, his rage cooling just slightly, replaced by a grim, calculating calm. He didn't need witnesses tonight. He didn't need to explain. Every punch had been a release, a reminder of why he was hunting Big Apple and everyone tied to him.

And as he stepped back, brushing off his hands, Detective Cross glanced down at his phone once more, eyes lingering on the pictures of the family he'd lost. His fists clenched again, quietly, silently promising that one day the fury that had just erupted over a careless bump would be nothing compared to what awaited Big Apple.

Chapter 6

Mac Ru leaned against the cold brick wall of the warehouse, his knuckles swollen and raw, every movement a reminder of the man he had beaten down the night before. Blood had dried beneath his fingernails, and though he had scrubbed them clean, the ache still pulsed through his hands like a drumbeat. That fight wasn't business—it was personal. The man had owed him money for too long, and when Mac Ru finally cornered him, there was no more talking. A debt unpaid was disrespect, and disrespect was something Mac Ru couldn't live with.

He flexed his fingers slowly, feeling the sting shoot up his forearm. Pain didn't bother him; it was almost a comfort, a reminder that he was still alive, still standing. But tonight wasn't about him. Tonight was about Savage.

The last time they had stood in this same warehouse, Savage had slid a heavy duffel bag across the concrete floor. Mac Ru remembered the sound it made when it landed with a solid thud. Money had a weight to it, a gravity that pulled men together and just as easily tore them apart. Inside that bag was $580,000 in crisp bills. Mac Ru hadn't trusted it at first. He had motioned to his lil homies—Knox, Dre, and Peanut—to count it up. They huddled over the stacks, licking their thumbs, whispering numbers as they laid the bands in neat towers.

Every bill was there. Savage didn't short him a dime. That was the first thing Mac Ru liked about him.

Savage wasn't like the other young wolves in the streets—reckless, loud, desperate to be seen. No, Savage was colder than most men twice his age. His eyes carried no hesitation, no remorse. He didn't laugh much, didn't brag, didn't waste words. He was young, yes, but heartless in a way that made even Mac Ru, a seasoned killer, pause.

Still, there was something about him Mac Ru respected. Maybe it was the way Savage handled business without emotions clouding the deal. Maybe it was how he looked Mac Ru in the eyes when he passed him nearly six hundred grand, like he was daring him to count it twice. Savage was dangerous, no doubt, but he was also disciplined. And discipline kept men alive longer than luck ever could.

That was months ago. And now, Savage was calling him in the middle of the night, voice edged with something Mac Ru had never heard from him before—rage rooted in grief.

Mac Ru lit a cigarette, the tip glowing in the dim light of the warehouse. Smoke curled from his lips as he thought back to Savage's words: Someone killed my family in cold blood.

Family. That was a line most men didn't cross, even in war. Business was one thing. Drugs, money, territory—those were fair game. But family? That was blood. That was sacred. Whoever had done it had written their death sentence in red ink.

The warehouse door creaked open, and footsteps echoed against the concrete. Mac Ru didn't flinch. He knew the sound—measured, confident. Savage stepped into view, dressed in all black, his face hard as stone.

"You came alone?" Mac Ru asked, flicking ash to the ground.

Savage nodded once. "Always."

Mac Ru studied him for a moment. His eyes were colder than usual, darker, as if the last bit of humanity in him had been carved out.

"Last time we was here, you dropped off a half a milli like it was nothin'," Mac Ru said, his voice low. "Now you call me talkin' 'bout blood on the floor. What happened?"

Savage didn't sit. He paced slowly, his fists clenching and unclenching. "They hit my people. Didn't just kill 'em. They wanted me to hurt. They left her laid out... like it was a message."

Mac Ru's jaw tightened. He had seen that kind of move before. It wasn't about money; it was about breaking a man's spirit. "You know who did it?"

Savage finally stopped pacing and looked at him dead-on. "Not yet. But I'm gonna find out. And when I do, they all gotta go. Not just the shooter. Everybody attached."

Mac Ru dragged on his cigarette, eyes narrowing. He could feel the young killer's fury radiating off him like heat. Savage wasn't bluffing; he never did. The kid would burn the city down brick by brick if it meant revenge.

"Careful," Mac Ru said evenly. "Anger makes you sloppy. You can't afford sloppy."

Savage smirked, but there was no humor in it. "Sloppy's for amateurs. I'm past that. This ain't rage, Mac. This is principle. They crossed a line. And lines don't get redrawn; they get erased."

For a moment, the warehouse fell silent, the only sound the faint hum of the city outside. Mac Ru flicked the cigarette butt to the floor, grinding it beneath his boot.

He thought back to the duffel bag, to the weight of $580,000 sitting at his feet. Money bought loyalty, sure. But this—this was different. This wasn't business Savage was asking him to step into. This was a war born from blood.

"You trust me enough to bring this to my table," Mac Ru said finally. "So here's what we do. You find out who dropped the hammer on your people. You bring me the name. When you do, I'll stand with you. We'll send a message back. One louder than theirs."

Savage's eyes didn't blink. "You mean that?"

Mac Ru held his stare. "I don't say shit I don't mean."

The younger man nodded once, then reached into his jacket. For a split second, Mac Ru's lil homies, Knox and

Dre, who had been lurking in the shadows, tensed up, hands on their steel. But Savage didn't pull a weapon. He pulled a folded photograph, creased from being carried too long. He handed it to Mac Ru.

It was a picture of Tasha, smiling wide, flashing a peace sign. Mac Ru studied it, then slid it back.

"That's why they all gotta go," Savage said, his voice barely above a whisper.

Mac Ru didn't argue. He couldn't.

The warehouse air grew heavier as the two men stood in silence, both knowing the next move would be painted in blood.

***

The warehouse was quiet except for the low hum of a space heater and the occasional drip of water from a busted pipe. Mac Ru sat in a metal chair, smoke curling from the blunt pinched between his fingers. The whole place smelled like dust, steel, and weed. Boxes stacked in the shadows gave the illusion of company, but he was alone with his thoughts—heavy thoughts.

Tasha's face floated in his mind, and it wasn't just because she was gone, but how she went out. Savage's cousin—blood to him, not to Mac Ru—but that didn't mean it didn't sting. He liked Tasha. She had a wild streak, sharp tongue, and enough ambition to chase money from angles most wouldn't dare. But that ambition cut both ways, and Mac Ru knew it. She set too many people up. She ran too many plays where the wrong name got dragged, the wrong man got robbed, and the wrong crew got hit.

In the streets, everybody has a limit. With K9, that limit had been crossed.

Mac Ru knew, even before word got around. K9 wasn't the type to let betrayal slide. Tasha had pushed too far, and K9 had dealt with it in the only way he knew—cold, fast, and final. One minute she was walking into a drop-off, probably smiling, thinking she was about to run another play. The next minute she was laid out on the ground, life leaking from her body while K9 walked away like it was just another Tuesday night.

That's what chilled Mac Ru. Not just the killing, but the calmness behind it. K9 killed like most men smoked cigarettes—casual, practiced, without thinking twice.

Mac Ru took a long drag on the blunt, eyes half-closed as the smoke filled his lungs. He thought about Savage. The kid didn't know yet—not the whole picture. He knew his cousin was gone, knew it was foul play, but the streets hadn't whispered K9's name in his ear. Not yet. Savage was hungry for answers, though, and Mac Ru respected that. There was something raw about him, something determined. Savage had the kind of fire you couldn't teach, the kind that made people either legends or ghosts before their time.

But Mac Ru also knew that chasing K9 without a plan was like stepping into traffic with your eyes closed. You missed your shot, and you weren't just dead—you were erased. K9's reach was long, his shooters loyal, his pockets deep. Taking him out was like signing your own death certificate if you didn't do it right.

Still, Mac Ru couldn't ignore that part of him that wanted to see it happen. K9 deserved it. He wasn't family, but he was poison in the streets, and Tasha's death was proof of it. So Mac Ru made himself a quiet promise as he exhaled another cloud of smoke into the warehouse air. If Savage dug deep enough to find the truth, if Savage put the pieces together and came to him with K9's name, Mac Ru would stand with him. He wouldn't just watch. He'd help.

Not because it was his blood. But because he liked Savage, saw something in him. And because in the back of his mind, he wanted to see K9 bleed too.

The blunt burned low in his fingers, and Mac Ru flicked the ash into an empty beer bottle on the floor. The warehouse stayed quiet, but his mind wasn't. He knew this story wasn't over. It was just waiting on Savage to make his move, and when he did, Mac Ru would be ready to put the murder one game down the way it was supposed to be played—smart, silent, and deadly.

***

Detective Cross stood in the cold silence of the cemetery, the autumn wind carrying with it the faint scent of damp leaves. The sky was a heavy gray, a blanket of clouds pressing down as though the heavens themselves shared in his grief. He moved slowly along the worn gravel path, the crunch beneath his boots sounding far too loud in a place meant for stillness. His eyes, tired and swollen from nights of restless thinking, locked onto the two headstones that stood side by side.

The names carved into stone never lost their sting. Elena Cross. Marcus Cross. His wife and his son. His heart ached the same way it did the day he first buried them. No amount of time had dulled it, no distraction had erased it. The pain was permanent, stitched into his very being.

He lowered himself to his knees, his breath hitching as his fingers traced the cold marble letters. His eyes blurred with tears, but he didn't wipe them away. He wanted his family to see him raw, unguarded.

"God, I miss you both," he whispered, his voice cracking. "Every damn day, I wake up reaching for you, Lena. I wake up hearing Marcus running through the halls, laughing, calling out for me to come play ball. And every morning, reality smacks me in the face, reminding me you're not here."

His chest heaved as sobs broke through. He leaned his forehead against his wife's headstone, his tears soaking into the chill stone. "You were my anchor, Lena. My reason to keep fighting in this ugly world. And Marcus… my little man… you were my light. And they ripped you away from me."

He clenched his fists, his nails digging into his palms until they hurt. The tears flowed harder, shoulders shaking, his cries muffled against the stone. The cemetery was empty, but he didn't care if the world heard his pain.

After a long silence, he sat back on his knees and looked up at the sky. His lips trembled. "I know who did this to you. I know who's responsible. And I swear on everything I have left, I will make him pay. He won't just feel the bullet; he'll feel the weight of what he stole from me. From us. He'll pay with his life, and I'll carry that burden gladly if it means justice for you."

His hands trembled as he reached for both headstones, one palm resting on his wife's, the other on his son's. "I'm sorry I couldn't protect you. I was supposed to keep you safe. That was my job, and I failed. But I won't fail again. Not in this."

Cross's breathing slowed, but the tears kept slipping down his face. He closed his eyes, letting the silence of the graveyard surround him. Then he began to whisper the words that had been etched into his soul since childhood: the Lord's Prayer. His voice shook, but every word carried the weight of his heart.

"Our Father, who art in heaven, hallowed be Thy name. Thy kingdom come, Thy will be done, on earth as it is in heaven…"

His voice broke halfway through, but he pressed on, his forehead once again lowering against the stone. "Give us this day our daily bread, and forgive us our trespasses, as we forgive those who trespass against us…" He clenched his jaw, knowing forgiveness wasn't something he had in his heart right now. Still, he whispered the words, hoping God would understand the storm raging inside him.

"And lead us not into temptation, but deliver us from evil. For Thine is the kingdom, and the power, and the glory, forever and ever. Amen."

Silence fell again, broken only by the faint rustle of leaves. Cross kept his hands on the stones, as if holding his family through the barrier of death.

"I love you both more than life," he whispered. "Nothing, not even death, can take that from me. I'll see you again. But before I do… I'll make sure the one who did this pays the price."

He kissed his fingertips and pressed them gently to each stone, lingering as if hoping to feel warmth return. Slowly, painfully, he stood, his legs stiff from kneeling. He looked down at the graves one last time, wiping his tears with the back of his hand, though more kept falling.

"I'll be back soon," he promised, voice low, firm. "But next time, I'll come with blood on my hands."

With that, Detective Cross turned and walked away, his shoulders heavy with grief, his heart burning with vengeance. The cemetery swallowed his footsteps, leaving only the whisper of the wind and the eternal silence of the dead.

Chapter 7

Symone's eyelids fluttered, heavy as though they'd been weighed down with lead. A faint white light pressed against them, not blinding, but soft and sterile. When she finally managed to open them, the world came into view blurry, then slowly sharpened. The ceiling was unfamiliar, lined with bright panels and faint hums of machinery. For a moment, panic rushed through her chest.

Her body screamed in pain. A dull ache radiated through her arms, her ribs, even her legs. She tried to shift, but every movement was like fire beneath her skin. "Oh my God," she whispered, the sound raw, her voice hoarse from disuse. She felt like she'd been buried alive, pulled from the edge of nothingness.

And then it hit her. Memories. All of it—flashes of blood, fear, the violence that had put her here. It was as if it had just happened yesterday. Her heart raced, her breath quickening, until she forced herself to calm down. She was alive. That much she knew. She was alive.

Blinking, she scanned the room. Balloons floated by the far wall, colorful against the cold, white hospital backdrop. Cards lined the windowsill and side tables, some propped up neatly, others leaning against each other. "Get Well Soon," "We Love You," "You're Strong." She could barely focus on the words, but she felt the warmth behind them.

Her eyes landed on the chair in the corner. A man slumped in it, head tilted back, arms crossed as though he'd been fighting sleep and lost. It was Test. His chest rose and fell in slow rhythm, exhaustion written all over his face. She wanted to cry just seeing him there. She knew Cash had put him on watch, keeping him here around the clock. She had been gone to the world, but not forgotten.

Tears welled in her eyes and slipped down her cheeks. She wasn't sure if they were from pain or gratitude, maybe both. Her lips parted, the sound fragile but enough to stir him.

"Test," she rasped.

His head jerked up instantly, his eyes wide, searching. He froze for half a heartbeat before rushing to her side. "Symone? Symone!" His hand clasped hers, warm and trembling. "Oh my God, you're awake."

She smiled faintly, weak but real. "I'm… alive."

"You damn right you are," Test said, voice breaking. "We've been waiting on this moment. Cash told me don't leave your side. He said, 'She gonna wake up, and when she do, I want somebody she know to be there.'" His eyes glistened. "And look at you now."

Before she could respond, the door opened and the doctor stepped in, a tall man with gray streaks in his hair, white coat pristine. He carried a clipboard, but his expression softened as he approached the bed.

"Well, well," he said with relief in his tone. "Miss Symone, you've decided to rejoin us."

She looked up at him, throat still raw. "How long I been here?" she whispered, the words more like a question than a statement.

He nodded. "You've been in a coma for just over eight weeks. But what matters is that you woke up—and you woke up with a miracle. You've been through something that should have taken your life, yet here you are. Your body has healed remarkably well. You're sore now, yes, but I want you to understand something: there's no permanent damage. No spinal injury, no brain trauma, nothing that should keep you from making a full recovery."

Her eyes widened. She couldn't believe it. After everything, after all that pain, she was going to walk away from this.

"How… how is that possible?" she asked.

The doctor smiled gently. "Sometimes medicine can't explain it all. You're one of the lucky ones. Someone up there must have been watching over you."

Test squeezed her hand tighter, nodding firmly. "Damn right. You hear that, Symone? You're blessed. Cash knew you was too strong to go out like that."

The doctor continued, his tone professional but warm. "It won't be easy. You'll need physical therapy, rest, and time. But you will recover. That's the important part. Today is the first day of the rest of your life." He placed the clipboard back under his arm and gave her a reassuring nod. "I'll give you two a moment."

As the doctor stepped out, Symone looked back at Test. Her lips trembled as she tried to form words. "I thought… I thought I was gone."

He shook his head fiercely. "Nah, don't talk like that. You're here. That's all that matters."

She let her eyes close for a second, feeling the weight of her survival press against her chest. The pain was real, the memories were sharp, but so was the love that surrounded her. Balloons, cards, Test's tired face, Cash's loyalty even in his absence.

She was alive. Against all odds, she was alive. And she silently promised herself she would never take another breath for granted.

***

The night is thick and mean, the kind of dark that feels alive. Rain spits against the cracked pavement, shining under the busted streetlights that blink on and off like they're half-asleep. Detective Cross sits in his car a block away, engine off, pistol resting heavy in his lap. He's not a cop tonight. He's not even a man tonight. He's a storm. A monster forged in grief.

His eyes don't blink much anymore, just fixed forward, cold as a corpse. He knows the soldier he's hunting—one of Big Apple's top boys, a Soulja Cash relies on for moving weight through this side of the city. Word is he's got five bricks in the trunk, ready to deliver before dawn. Cross doesn't need the coke. But he needs the message. He needs the blood.

He slides out the car, hoodie up, and melts into the shadows. The block is quiet, just the hum of streetlights and the occasional hiss of tires through rainwater. Cross moves like a shadow with a heartbeat, boots soft on the wet ground. He spots the soldier—a tall, mean-looking dude with a leather jacket and a gold chain swinging on his chest—standing by a black Charger parked half crooked. Cigarette glowing in his mouth, gun tucked lazy in his waistband. He's waiting on somebody. That's his mistake. Waiting.

Cross doesn't rush. He stalks. Every step is measured. His breath slow, calm, like he's already at peace with what's about to happen. The soldier takes another drag, flicks ash, never noticing the death sliding toward him.

Then it happens. Cross steps out of the dark, fast and mean. Gun comes up, black steel catching what little light there is. "Don't move."

The soldier freezes, cigarette halfway to his lips. His hand twitches toward his waist. Cross fires. One shot to the thigh, ripping meat and bone, dropping the man screaming to the wet pavement.

The sound is loud in the night, echoing off the brick walls. But Cross doesn't care. He's past caring. He rushes in, boots stomping, and smashes the gun across the soldier's face, cracking skin, breaking teeth. Blood sprays with the rain.

"Big Apple," Cross growls, voice low, shaking with rage. "He killed my family. You ride for him? You die for him."

The soldier spits blood, tries to crawl. Cross grabs him by the jacket and slams his head against the concrete once, twice, three times—until his skull makes that wet thud, until the fight leaks out of him. The man gasps, choking on rain and blood, eyes rolling.

Cross kneels over him, pressing the barrel against his mouth. "Tell him I'm coming."

The soldier gurgles, lips trembling around the steel. Cross pulls the trigger. The back of his skull explodes against the sidewalk, spraying the dark with red.

For a moment, Cross just kneels there, staring at the body twitching in the puddle, blood mixing with rain, turning the water pink. His chest rises and falls heavy, but his face is stone. No remorse. No hesitation. Just a hollow man carrying a death sentence for everyone tied to Big Apple.

He wipes the gun against the dead man's jacket, stands, and pops the Charger's trunk. Plastic-wrapped bricks sit neat and ready, smelling like money and power. Cross grabs all five, tossing them into a duffel he pulled from his backseat earlier. He zips it shut, slings it over his shoulder.

Before he leaves, he kneels again, takes the soldier's chain, and rips it off his neck. A trophy. A warning.

The rain is harder now, pounding the pavement, washing away some of the blood but not all. The body looks like a broken doll under the light. Cross stares down at it one last time. "One down," he whispers. "Apple, I'll carve my way to you piece by piece."

He slips back into the night, duffel heavy on his shoulder, pistol ready in his hand. The war has started.

***

The hospital smells like antiseptic and sadness. Cash steps quietly into Symone's room, hands shoved deep into the pockets of his hoodie. She's lying there, pale, hooked up to a tangle of tubes and monitors, the steady beep of the heart machine filling the silence. Flowers crowd the bedside table, cards leaning against each other, balloons floating lazily from the ceiling. Symone shifts, eyes fluttering open, and he feels his chest tighten.

"Hey," he says softly, pulling a chair up next to her bed. "You feeling any better?"

Symone manages a weak smile, her throat dry, voice barely a whisper. "Better… I think."

Cash watches her for a long moment, noting the bruises, the cuts, the way her arm twitches involuntarily. He knows she's been through hell. Two months in a coma, and now she's finally waking up. He wishes he could erase all the pain, but life doesn't work like that.

"You scared me," he admits, his hand brushing the hair off her forehead. "You don't know how much I was worried."

Symone's eyes glisten. "I remember… everything. It feels… like it just happened yesterday."

He nods, trying to push down the guilt that claws at him every time he looks at her. He's supposed to be the protector, the one keeping everyone alive, but there's only so much a man can do. Still, he's here now, and that has to count for something.

For a few minutes, they sit in silence. The machines beep steadily, the rain tapping against the window outside, the world outside this room moving and breathing while inside it feels frozen. Cash leans back, letting the tension leave his shoulders for just a second, savoring this small victory.

Then his phone buzzes.

He frowns, fishing it out of his pocket. The number flashing isn't familiar, but that doesn't matter. He answers on the second ring.

"Yo?"

The voice on the other end is sharp, urgent. "Boss… one of the hitters you know, the one moving the pack tonight?

He's gone. Dead. Someone hit him, took the bricks. Five kilos."

Cash freezes. The words hit him like a punch to the gut. His hand tightens around the phone, knuckles whitening. "What the fuck you mean, gone?"

"Some dude," the voice continues, almost shaking, "he came outta nowhere. Didn't leave a trace. The guy's clean. We lost him, boss."

Cash swallows hard. His eyes flick to Symone. She's looking at him, confused, sensing the sudden shift in his mood. He can't let her see it—not yet. Not while she's recovering. He slides the phone out of her line of sight and mutters, "I'll handle it."

But inside, the rage is building, slow and cold. He can feel it crawl up his spine, sinking into his chest like molten lead. Someone dared to touch him, someone dared to disrespect his empire while he was busy looking after this girl. And now, that disrespect has to be answered.

Symone reaches for his hand, eyes wide. "Cash… what's wrong?"

He squeezes her hand quickly, forcing a calm that isn't really there. "Nothing. Just… business stuff. Forget it."

But he can't forget it. He won't. The memory of that soldier's body, the missing five kilos, the audacity of the hit—it's fire in his veins now, unstoppable. He knows exactly who can pull this off. Someone smart, cold, and precise. Someone who wants to start a war.

Cash pulls the phone back, tapping it against his palm, thinking fast. "Get every camera on the block. I want faces. I want names. I want whoever did this caught."

The voice hesitates, almost scared. "Boss… you think it's one of them? Snake Eyes' peoples?"

Cash doesn't answer immediately. The name burns in his ears. Snake Eyes. That man has been a ghost in the streets lately—too careful, too patient. To a war that already started.

He looks back at Symone, sitting weak but alive. She's the reason he's still human, the only thing keeping him from going completely savage right now. But this… this attack? It's personal now. It's on him.

"I'll find him," Cash says finally, voice low and deadly. "And whoever's with him? They're next."

He hangs up and sets the phone on the bedside table, staring out the rain-streaked window. The world feels different now, heavier, darker. This isn't just about the money or the empire anymore. This is about respect. About revenge. About survival.

Symone stirs again, and he glances back, trying to force a smile. "You rest," he says softly. "I'll handle the rest."

But inside, he's already planning. Every move, every strike, every shot. The city is about to bleed, and he'll make sure the first drop is felt by the people who thought they could touch him.

Cash leans back, taking a deep breath, and lets the cold rage sink fully in. This isn't just another hit. This is war. And Snake Eyes is a fucking dead man walking.

Chapter 8

Cash's voice echoes off the concrete walls of the warehouse, booming and violent. "Who the fuck did this?" he yells, fists slamming against a crate so hard it rattles the pallets around him. Sweat drips down his face, his eyes wide with rage, fire burning in every vein. "I want answers *now*!"

His crew stands frozen, some shrinking back, some exchanging nervous glances. Nobody dares speak. The tension is thick, almost choking. Cash's breathing is heavy, like a predator circling its prey, his anger radiating so strong it's almost visible.

"Y'all think this some joke?" he screams, pacing like a caged lion. "My Soulja is dead, and y'all act like it ain't shit!" His voice cracks, raw with grief and fury, bouncing off the walls, making the metal shelves shiver.

Cash grabs the nearest guy by the collar, slamming him into a stack of boxes. "Where were you when this shit went down? Huh?" The man stammers, eyes wide, hands raised, barely able to breathe. Cash's knuckles whiten as he shakes him violently. "I ain't playing, motherfucker!"

Then, without warning, Cash kicks a crate across the floor. The contents—a pile of stolen goods from the Soulja hit—spill everywhere. He yells louder now, a mix of vengeance and desperation. "And you motherfuckers stole from him too?!"

His crew flinches, knowing every word cuts like a knife.

He stops, chest heaving, and glares at everyone in the warehouse. His voice drops, low and deadly. "If I find out who did this… there ain't gonna be nothin' left for 'em to remember." His eyes scan the room, narrowing, seeing every twitch, every nervous glance.

Cash moves to the middle of the chaos, the stolen kilos of cocaine at his feet, and picks up one, weighing it in his hand. "This right here," he growls, "this is blood money. You stole blood money. And I swear, whoever touched it… I'm gonna make 'em pay with everything they got. And I mean everything."

He throws the bag across the warehouse. It hits the wall, bursting open. Powder scatters like snow on the floor. Cash stands over it, towering, rage still boiling. "Y'all better start talkin'," he says, voice low, deadly calm now, "or I swear I'll start takin' heads one by one."

Silence. Except for Cash's heavy breathing and the soft, helpless shuffle of his crew. No one moves. They know better than to test him.

Then Cash grabs a metal pipe off the floor and swings it, letting it clang against a steel support beam. Sparks fly. His eyes glint. "I don't care if it's family, friends, whoever… if I don't get answers, I'll bury all of y'all in this warehouse myself!"

The crew finally starts talkin', pointing fingers, whispering names. Cash's rage doesn't lessen; if anything, it feeds off their fear. Every whispered accusation hits him like gasoline on fire.

Cash's voice rises again, louder than before, shaking the rafters. "I told y'all! I warned y'all! My Soulja is dead! And I'm gonna make sure whoever did this pays in ways you can't even imagine!"

He stops talking, chest heaving, dripping with sweat. His eyes scan the chaos, glinting like steel. One thought dominates his mind: revenge. Every last person involved will pay. Every single one.

***

The engine of Mac Ru's black-on-black BMW hummed low as they cruised down the city streets, speakers rattling with Lil Baby's latest track. Smoke curled around the cabin from the blunt resting between Mac Ru's fingers. Savage tapped ash into the cupholder, his eyes flicking to Mac Ru through the haze.

"K9?" Mac Ru finally broke the silence, exhaling slow. "We only got one shot at this, you feel me?"

Savage nodded, jaw tight. "Yeah, I know. One fuckin' shot. We can't fuck it up. Dude don't see it coming."

Mac Ru flicked the smoke toward the dashboard, watching it swirl. "He think he untouchable. Plays with the wrong folks, but he don't even know we watchin'. Every move he make, we know."

Savage leaned back, rubbing his hands together. "So how we do this? Straight-up ambush, or we make it look like somethin' else?"

Mac Ru's grin was cold. "Nah, we play smart. Set him up where he don't expect it. Get him alone, make it clean. No witnesses, no mistakes. One fuckin' chance, Savage. One chance to send him out the game."

Savage nodded, heart thumping. "I got you. I ain't scared. Just tell me what I gotta do."

Mac Ru leaned forward, voice dropping to a whisper over the music. "We gotta watch his moves, see his routine. Don't rush. Wait for the right moment. One slip, and it's over for us." He took another drag, letting the smoke fill the car. "This ain't no game, Savage. One fuckin' shot, that's it. You ready?"

Savage's eyes hardened. "Born ready. Let's set this motherfucker up and finish it."

The car slid through the streets, speakers booming, smoke thick—two killers planning their one shot, cold, calculated, and ready to move when the time was right.

***

K9 sat in the corner of the warehouse, the fluorescent lights buzzing overhead, casting cold, flickering shadows across the room. The air smelled of powder, sweat, and money—five million dollars in fresh bills stacked on the long metal table in front of him. His right-hand man, Big T, moved quickly, counting the bundles with precision, double-checking every stack, every strap. The sound of the bills thudding against the metal table echoed through the empty space, mixing with the low hum of the old ceiling fan above.

"Damn, K9," Big T muttered, shaking his head as he moved another strap into place. "This shit's heavy… but, yo, bodies droppin' everywhere. Cash hittas been busy out there."

K9's eyes didn't leave the table. He traced the edges of the stacks with a finger, counting silently, his mind elsewhere. "I know," he said finally, voice low but sharp. "Snake Eyes talkin' shit, wantin' to strike back for his man. But it ain't just him. Everyone out here actin' like this street shit ain't dangerous. Bodies droppin' in the five boroughs, and my money stoppin'."

Big T hesitated, glancing at the stacks and then at K9, reading the tension behind his calm exterior. "Word is Cash ain't done. He got more boys out there. We can't keep having bodies drop and expect the money to keep flowin'."

K9 slammed his hand on the table, rattling the bills. "Cash and Snake Eyes is fucking my money up. I'm ready to bury both of them," he said, eyes burning with intensity. "But we gotta be smart. Every move counts. Every hitter needs to be on point. Bodies droppin', yeah… but the money? That's life. And right now, life's slippin' fast."

Big T nodded, but the tension in his shoulders didn't ease. "A'ight, boss. But you know the streets don't wait for nobody. Every night it's somethin'. Bodies, rumors, money stoppin'… people get nervous."

K9 leaned back in his chair, lighting a cigarette, letting the smoke curl into the flickering light above. He took a long drag, exhaling slow, and let the haze fill the room like a warning. "Nervous? Yeah, people nervous. But I don't run scared. You know that. We move smart, we move calculated. Ain't nobody stopping my money. Not Cash, not Snake Eyes, not no one."

Big T's eyes flicked toward the stacks again. "So what we do? We beef up security, double the hitters on patrol?"

"Patrol? You think patrol gon' save us if the police come?" K9's voice was low, dangerous. "We gotta watch the corners, watch the traps. Whoever thinkin' they can say fuck my orders? We hit first. You feel me? Bodies droppin', yeah, but that ain't the problem. Problem is lettin' folks know they ain't gettin' a free pass here."

He stood and started pacing, boots echoing off the concrete floor. "Every shipment gotta be tight, every move gotta be calculated. We keepin' eyes on the streets, on the boys, on everybody. Trust nobody too much. Friends out here? They temporary. Enemies? They permanent. That's how it work."

Big T swallowed, nodding along, tension thick in the air. "A'ight, boss. We got you. We'll move smart. Keep the money flowin', keep the streets quiet."

K9 stopped pacing and turned, eyes blazing. "Quiet? Nah, streets never quiet. Streets screamin' every night, every block. You gotta listen, feel it, read it. Bodies droppin', money slowin', rumors spreadin'. That's the pulse of this city, and if you ain't payin' attention, you gon' die."

He lit another cigarette, inhaling deep, letting the smoke curl around his face like armor. "Cash out there killin' Snake Eyes' boys, Snake Eyes wantin' revenge… everybody tryna play the boss. But I ain't no rookie. I see moves before they happen. I see snakes before they strike. And I strike first when I gotta. That's the only way a real boss moves."

Big T shifted nervously, eyeing the stacks again. "And the money?"

"The money?" K9 snapped, voice sharp. "Money's power. Lose the money, you lose control. Lose control, you lose everything. Five million right here, yeah, it's heavy, it's life… but it ain't just numbers. It's loyalty, respect, fear. It's proof that we still run shit. And I ain't lettin' nobody take that from me."

He leaned over the table, hands brushing the stacks like a king claiming his crown. "Get every hitter on overtime. Watch every move. Keep eyes on every block. Watch Cash, watch Snake Eyes, watch the streets. Don't slip. One wrong move? One shot we miss? And it's over. Bodies droppin', yeah… but if I lose my empire? I ain't comin' back from that."

Big T nodded, swallowing hard. "We got you, K9. Ain't nobody takin' your spot."

K9 exhaled smoke slowly, the warehouse thick with tension and the scent of money. Outside, the city never slept, and neither did the threats. Cash was moving, Snake Eyes was scheming, and every step K9 took had to be calculated, precise. One slip, one betrayal, one mistake… and this empire could crumble.

But K9? He wasn't worried. Not yet.

Chapter 9

He sits at the kitchen table with the light low and the city humming like a beast beyond the blinds. The lamp throws a yellow pool across the Formica where magazines, a rag, and the gun lay like the props of a life he can't deny. Detective Cross moves slow and sure, a man who remembers what it feels like when time goes thin and rage sits heavy in your chest. He wipes the barrel without thinking about mechanics, thinking instead about the black-and-white photos tacked to the wall across from him: Big Apple's face a dozen times, different angles, different nights. He's enlarged one of them, taped it to the center like a target that won't have to be paper for long.

A bottle of Cîroc sits to his right, condensation running down the glass. He takes a pull, lets the burn settle like an old friend, then sets the bottle down with a little too much care. The rhythm of his hands is almost meditative—wipe, stroke, check the chamber—but his eyes keep cutting back to the wall. In each photo, Big Apple smiles like he owns the street. In Cross's head, the smile warps into something else: a promise, a ledger, the account that won't balance until blood pays the debt.

He pours a line of cocaine across the table like a bright, dangerous stripe. It catches the light, and for a second the room looks like a stage. He hesitates, eyes closing, then snorts a thin line, quick and clinical. It sharpens him—not in the way the badge used to, not by the book, but in a raw, animal way. The edge it gives him is clean and cruel. He hates it and he loves it both exactly the same. The small white rush pushes the ache away and gives him room to breathe plans into existence.

"First I crash their world," he says to the empty apartment, to the pictures, to the ghost of his family that still lives in the corners. The words are not bravado. They are a blueprint he repeats until the lines feel like steel. He's not thinking in single bullets or a single moment with Big Apple in the crosshairs. He wants collapse—*infrastructure and loyalty and money.* He wants Big Apple brought down so that when he finally takes the man, there's nowhere for him to hide.

The bottle feels cold in his fingers. He drinks slow now, measuring the burn. He remembers the day his wife and son were murdered. He remembers the way the precinct looked at him after, with pity in their eyes and fear in their mouths. They called it collateral. He calls it a debt.

Cross sets the rag aside and rubs the palm of his hand over his forehead until he feels the skin prickle. The room spins for a second, sharp and steady, and the portraits blur. He steadies the glass with an elbow and smiles a small, brutal smile. He's been a cop long enough to know how to mask the thing inside him. He's been a human long enough to know there's no mask for what he's about to do.

Outside, a siren keens and then fades. Inside, the only sound is the clink of the bottle and the whisper of cloth on metal. He looks at the framed photograph—his family, years earlier—and the image is a kind of compass. He pins it with one thumb on the table, as if the life he loved can be used as ballast. Underneath it, his phone buzzes once, a message he doesn't open. It can wait. Plans like his need room to breathe, room to eddy, to gather all the other men with holes in their chests.

He thinks about the crews that orbit Big Apple: the runners, the lookouts, the men who would sell their sisters for a nod. Take the money, take the stash houses, take the men who think themselves safe because they sleep with bullets tucked in their boots and loyalty in their mouths. Crush their supply lines, burn their safe houses, make the ground under their feet move. When the men who work for Big Apple wake up and find there's no money, no dope, no habit to feed, they'll start looking for answers, for someone to blame. He doesn't want them pointing their fingers at him; he wants them pointing at the emptiness he leaves in his wake.

He drums his fingers on the table. The idea excites a cold part of his brain—not the part that used to write reports and file warrants, but the animal that kept him alive on nights when he walked a block and listened to every shadow. He's not naïve enough to think the law will help him. The law failed him. The law is softer than a whisper now. So he will become an earthquake: not targeted at one man first, but at the whole system that let monsters like Big Apple crawl free in the daylight.

Cross reaches up and pats the weapon's side as if to steady both. The gun is not a sermon; it's an implement, a promise. He won't rush the final act. He will wait until Big Apple's world has imploded upon itself like rotten timber. Then he'll step out and finish what nights and ghosts began.

He snorts another thin line. The taste is metallic and sharp, and it clears the last fog. In his head, the city already smolders—safe houses raided, men found sleeping at their tables with their throats cut, accounts looted, loyalties bought and broken. He imagines Big Apple learning the geography of loss: his men gone, his product gone, his money evaporated. The thought is a small joy, cruel and absolute.

Someone once told him that vengeance is a banquet, not a snack. Cross sets his jaw and pushes his chair back. The rag flutters to the floor. He stands with the light weighing on his shoulders and the photos glaring like witnesses. He picks up the bottle, drinks until it's only a memory of cold, and then tucks the gun into the back of his waistband like a secret prayer.

"You want the body count?" he says quietly, to the room, to the photos, to no one at all. "I'll give you the collapse first."

He steps toward the wall and circles the central photo with a single marker stroke, a small black ring he didn't plan but now can't unmake. The ring is a beginning, or an end. Cross turns the light off, and the apartment falls into the thin, patient dark, the street outside keeping its slow, murderous rhythm.

In the dark, Detective Cross listens to the city breathe and counts the ways he'll make it scream.

The warehouse breathes city heat—oil on concrete, a faint chemical tang, the hum of a neon sign through cracked windows. A soldier with a scarred jaw eases the rolling door up, rubber scraping like a soft warning. Tires whisper on stained pavement. The black Cadillac Escalade rolls in slow, chrome catching the light, and the soldier jerks his chin toward the passenger door.

K9 steps out like he owns the dark. He's wearing a fitted coat, a Cuban cigar clenched between two fingers, smoke already forming a thin halo that smells of spice and money. He strolls up the center aisle like a man who's staggered through every borough and kept his balance. Men in the corners fall quiet; even the rats in the rafters seem to hush.

Cash stands under a single bare bulb, all leather and shadow. He watches K9 the way a hunter watches the wind—patient, unreadable. They close the distance, and the handshake is long and honest, palm to palm, a pact they both know how to keep. The handshake breaks, but their hands don't instantly let go; a small, human hesitation that says too much.

"Good to see you, K9," Cash says low.

"You too," K9 replies, voice smooth as the cigar smoke. "You look well."

They walk toward the office, away from the men, away from the clocks. The soldier shuts the heavy door behind them and flips the chain. Inside the private room, the air feels thicker, like the walls have been fed rumors and promises. K9 takes a slow draw from his cigar, the ember flaring orange in the dim.

"I'm gonna be straight," K9 says, and his eyes don't move from Cash. "There's too many bodies. The streets been talking, and when streets talk, they bring ears. FBI. DEA. Local PD. They start sniffin' close. We can't have that. You can't have that."

Cash leans back in the chair, fingers tapping the wood. "Sometimes motherfuckers only respect violence," he says. "Snake Eyes—he's one of them. You kill my man, I kill yours. Money keep moving, business keep moving. Murder's part of the life. We do what we gotta do."

K9 snorts, slow and unimpressed. He gestures with the cigar, a cathedral of smoke. "I been in this long, Cash. Longer than most. I built out from nothing, made millions, hundreds if you wanna talk big numbers. I got friends in places you don't wanna visit. I listen to them. I learn." He folds his hands, laying a map of intent on the table without touching it. "I back what you do. I supply what you need. But you hearing me?"

Cash watches the ember, watches K9 watching him. He doesn't reach for the cigar. He doesn't smile. He listens the way a man counts bullets—careful, slow.

"So let me be clear, respectfully," K9 continues, slow and clean. "The next person that steps outta line, whether that person's you or that Snake Eyes fool, they gonna be U.E."

Cash's face stays still. The room takes the breath from his chest and holds it.

"You know what that means," K9 adds, words soft as velvet, teeth on a razor. "Under the Earth. No questions. No bodies showing up later in alleys. Disappeared proper. Respectfully, you work for me. You understand that, yes?"

Cash's jaw moves once, small. He doesn't say the words back. He doesn't need to. In the warehouse, those two syllables—*work for me*—are more than a line on a ledger. They're the hinge on which lives swing.

"One of your soldiers get outta line, you kill 'em." K9 leans in a hair, making the logic sharp. "You get outta line, I kill you. Respectfully."

K9's voice is velvet; his promise is iron. He flicks ash into a glass ashtray and stands.

"I got a talk to have with Snake Eyes next," he says. "I don't like bringin' this, but I got to. Too much heat, Cash. Too many eyes. You fix your side, I fix mine. We move forward clean."

Cash says nothing. He watches K9 button his coat, watches the slow tilt of his head as if to say this conversation is over but the warning remains. The soldier at the door opens it again. Night rushes in wet and alive.

K9 steps into the light, the cigar still a red promise at his lip. He turns his head just once to look at Cash, the kind of look that counts debts and reads intentions. "Be careful," he says, the words carrying less like advice and more like a verdict.

Then he's gone, swallowed by the hush of the street and the Escalade's growl. The garage door closes heavy behind him, and the warehouse exhales.

Cash sits alone under the bulb for a long time after the room slips back into its usual noise. Men move, machines hum, business resumes like a pulse. He picks up the ashtray, studies the grey nub of K9's cigar, and taps the ash until it scatters on the table.

Respect. He respects the man's reach. He respects the caution. But respect don't equal obedience.

He stands, walks to the small window, and watches the taillights disappear into the night. He presses his palms to the glass, feeling the city on the other side—quick, dangerous, hungry. He doesn't answer with words. He answers with silence that contains an ocean of decisions.

Outside, the street keeps counting breaths, feet, and the slow, certain drip of time. Inside, Cash turns away from the window and starts to plan.

The block is quiet enough to make every sound carry.

A gust moves the trash on the curb, a loose newspaper lifts and skates across the pavement. Inside Cash's warehouse, the rolling door drops shut and seals the talk between bosses. A black Cadillac Escalade glides back into the open air, headlights catching dust that floats like snow in the beam.

Across the street, two men sit in a parked car that doesn't belong on this side of town. The windows are up, the music off. Mac Ru leans forward, resting his forearms on the wheel. Savage sits back, chewing on a toothpick, watching the warehouse like he's studying a test he already knows the answers to.

"That's him," Mac Ru says quietly.

Savage nods. "K9."

They both fall silent again, the weight of a shared memory hanging between them—the nights when Tasha's name was still a heartbeat, when revenge wasn't an idea but a promise whispered in smoke.

The Escalade rolls down the block slow, cautious, like it's aware that silence can be a setup. The men inside are laughing, though; they think the night belongs to them. Mac Ru starts the engine. It doesn't roar; it hums, tuned for discretion.

Savage checks the street, then looks back at Mac Ru.

"You sure you wanna do this now?"

Mac Ru's jaw flexes. "If not now, when?"

They pull out, trailing the Cadillac from half a block behind. Streetlights blink through the windshield in rhythm, the city breathing through flickers of yellow and red. The air feels heavy, like the block is holding its breath.

At the next intersection, Mac Ru hits the turn and slides the car sideways, cutting across the lane. The Cadillac hesitates, brake lights flashing. For a heartbeat, everything freezes. Two worlds—power and payback—stare each other down through glass and steel.

Mac Ru's voice is low. "Let's finish what we started."

Then sound erupts—not from the muzzle flash or the chaos, but from the wind that follows it, the echo that makes every dog in the neighborhood bark. Windows up and down the street flare with light as people duck, close curtains, pretend they didn't hear what they heard. Tires screech. A horn blares and dies.

By the time the noise fades, the air smells like burnt metal and panic. The Cadillac lists against the curb, smoke curling from beneath its hood. One of the doors swings open a few inches and then hangs still. The other car—Mac Ru's—is already gone, disappearing into the narrow veins of the city where headlights vanish faster than secrets.

For a moment, the block is empty again, like it's trying to rewrite itself back to peace. But the silence doesn't last. Somewhere nearby, sirens answer the call that no one made.

Inside the Cadillac, the world is red and spinning. K9 blinks against the taste of copper, his thoughts stumbling over one another, trying to make sense of the ambush. He can feel heat on his skin, hear someone calling his name. His second-in-command slumps forward, voice ragged, trying to keep K9 conscious.

"Stay with me, boss… we good, we good…"

The words sound far away.

K9 tries to move, but the world sways with him. He presses a palm against his chest and feels warmth he doesn't want to name. His mind flickers between moments—the warehouse talk, Cash's steady stare, the smell of that cigar—and a quiet realization begins to bloom in the center of his chest: somebody ain't listening anymore.

Headlights bloom again. A car screeches to a stop behind the ruined Escalade. Two of K9's own soldiers jump out, weapons drawn, scanning the shadows. They see the mess, see their boss, and every line of their faces hardens into disbelief. One of them yells for help while the other yanks open the passenger door.

"Boss, we got you. Hold on!"

The sound of distant sirens grows louder. Somebody calls an ambulance, somebody else calls a cleanup crew, somebody curses Cash's name, though no one's said it was him. The rumors are already getting out before anyone checks the facts.

At Saint Vernon Hospital, the corridors blur with motion—nurses pushing carts, security shouting codes, men in expensive coats pacing under flickering lights. K9's crew floods the waiting area, cell phones buzzing with rumors and half-truths.

One of the soldiers, a tall man named Royce, leans against the wall, eyes red, phone to his ear.

"We don't know who yet," he says. "All I know, the boss got hit bad. Chest, shoulder. He's breathin', but he's out. They workin' on him now."

Another man slams a fist into the vending machine. "Snake Eyes?" he growls.

Royce shakes his head. "Could be. Could be Cash. Could be anybody who think they tough enough."

The tension vibrates through the hall like static. Every phone call adds more noise, more names, more blame.

Inside the operating room, K9 drifts between darkness and the steady beeping of machines. Faces float above him—doctors, nurses, fragments of light. He hears himself say something but can't remember what. The only clear thought that survives the haze is the memory of Cash's eyes, calm and unreadable. *Respectfully,* K9 had said. The word now tastes like irony.

Chapter 10

Mac Ru and Savage sit in an underground garage, the car cooling in the corner. They don't speak for a long time. The only sound is the tick of the engine settling. Savage finally exhales, long and low.

"You think he's dead?"

Mac Ru wipes sweat from his temple. "Don't matter. Message sent."

Savage shakes his head. "Yeah, but that message just lit a fire we can't put out."

Mac Ru looks up, eyes hard. "Fire was already burning. We just made sure they saw the smoke."

He steps out of the car, walks a few paces toward the mouth of the garage, and stares at the skyline—a smear of lights and noise. Somewhere out there, police radios are screaming, and someone is already making a list of suspects. He knows Cash's name will be on it. He knows Snake Eyes will smell blood and opportunity. And he knows the city will never stop watching once it tastes fresh chaos.

Savage joins him. "What now?"

"Now," Mac Ru says, "we vanish. Let the streets talk. Let everybody guess who did what. By the time they figure it out, it'll be too late to fix it."

They watch the city for another minute. The sounds from far away—sirens, shouts, tires on wet asphalt—roll through the tunnels like thunder. Savage turns to leave first.

Back at the hospital, the hallway doors swing open and a doctor steps out, face unreadable. The crew jumps to their feet. Royce speaks first.

"How is he?"

The doctor hesitates. "He's alive," he says finally. "For now. But he'll need time."

The men exhale all at once, half relief, half rage. Someone mutters that whoever did this won't see another sunrise. Someone else whispers Cash's name again. The rumor takes shape, small and dangerous.

K9's phone sits on a tray beside his hospital bed, screen lighting up with unanswered messages. One of them is from Snake Eyes:

"Heard what happened. We need to talk. S.E."

The city outside hums like it always does, pretending it didn't just watch a king bleed. But the rules have changed. Respect is about to be redefined, one quiet move at a time.

Chapter 11

The rain hadn't let up all day. It beat down on the tin roof of Cash's warehouse like a slow war drum, steady and mean. Inside, the air was thick with the smell of diesel, gun oil, and tension. Stacks of boxes lined the walls, some sealed, others cracked open, showing bricks of white powder wrapped in plastic.

Cash stood at the long metal table in the center of the floor. A single light bulb hung above him, casting a hard yellow glow that cut through the shadows. A half-empty bottle of Hennessy sat beside a stripped-down Glock, the pieces spread like a puzzle only he could solve. Cleaning it wasn't about the gun; it was about keeping his hands busy while his mind spun.

The warehouse door creaked open. Footsteps echoed on the concrete before a familiar voice called out.

"Yo, you in here, Cash?"

"Yeah," Cash said without looking up. "Come through."

Big Apple stepped out of the shadows, raindrops sliding off his black hoodie. He glanced around before locking eyes with Cash.

"Heard you was in here thinkin'," Big Apple said, his tone low. "Figured I'd slide through before things get any louder out there."

Cash slid the barrel back into place, slow and steady. "Word movin' that fast?"

"Faster than ever," Apple said, leaning on the table. "Word on the street people say you the one sent that hit at K9. They say he fightin' for his life right now. Snake Eyes already rallyin' his people. Everybody talkin' like war's already called."

Cash said nothing. He poured another drink, ice crackin' in the glass. "Crazy how fast a lie move when truth ain't around to defend itself."

"Yeah," Apple muttered. "But truth don't stop bullets. You know that. Streets react first, ask questions at funerals."

The air tightened between them. Big Apple wasn't accusing him; he was warning him. Cash could hear the worry under the rough tone.

"I ain't put no greenlight on K9," Cash said finally. "Not yet. I was thinkin' about it, but I didn't move. Whoever did that just lit a fuse we can't put out."

Apple nodded. "Then somebody playin' chess while we still tryin' to figure the board. And if K9 don't make it, every soldier he ever fed gon' look at you like you did it."

Cash stared at the drink in his hand. "I know. That's the part that burn me. Somebody usin' my name to start a war. I built this off loyalty, off respect. Now they tryna flip that against me. They want chaos."

Apple started pacing, heavy boots echoing on the floor. "You gotta think, Cash—who benefits from this? Who's pushin' that story? Snake Eyes talkin', yeah, but he don't move this fast unless somebody feedin' him info. Somebody close."

Cash looked up sharp. "You sayin' we got a leak?"

"I'm sayin' it look that way," Apple replied. "How else they know about moves that never even happened? How they tie it to you unless somebody inside whispered it?"

Cash set his glass down hard. "A rat. In my circle. That's the last thing I need right now."

"Then don't move reckless," Apple said. "That's what they want. You start swingin' wild, you look guilty. You prove 'em right."

Cash rubbed a hand down his face, thinking. "So what you suggest?"

Apple shrugged. "Sit still but stay ready. Watch who call who. Watch who go ghost. Keep your loyal ones close, but don't tell nobody what you plannin'. Not even me, unless it's time."

A beat passed. The rain tapped steady on the windows.

"You sound like you know somethin'," Cash said. "You holdin' out?"

Apple smirked faintly. "If I knew, you'd already have names. But I feel it. The air different, bro. This ain't just K9's people tryna spin the block. Somebody orchestratin' this. Somebody want everybody at each other's throats so they can slide in clean when the dust settle."

Cash's eyes drifted around the warehouse—money, product, power, all of it built from the ground up. For the first time, it looked fragile.

"You ever feel like we movin' in circles?" Cash asked quietly. "Like no matter how far ahead we get, somebody always drag us back to the same war?"

Apple gave a small laugh with no humor in it. "That's the life we chose. You can't have power without enemies. You just gotta make sure the enemies don't come disguised as brothers."

Cash picked up the Glock, snapped the slide back, and chambered a round. The metallic click filled the room.

"Ain't nobody catchin' me slippin'," he said. "I'ma play it cool, keep the business movin', but I'm watchin' everything. If this turn into a war, we endin' it quick."

Apple's brow furrowed. "You sure you ready for that? Once the first shot go off, there ain't no turnin' back."

Cash's stare didn't waver. "Ain't been no turnin' back since the first brick I sold."

The words sat heavy in the space between them. Outside, thunder rolled. Inside, only the hum of the overhead bulb filled the silence.

"You ever wonder how long this lasts?" Cash asked. "Us movin' like this? Every day could be the one that close the chapter."

"It lasts as long as you keep control," Apple said. "Lose that, you lose everything. Respect, money, power—they all built on fear. And right now, fear's what's keepin' the streets quiet."

Cash nodded slowly. His jaw tightened. "Then I guess it's time I remind the streets what fear really look like."

Apple didn't answer right away. He just looked at Cash—the man he'd watched rise from a corner hustler to a name the city whispered. He saw something different in his eyes now. Not anger. Calculation.

"Alright," Apple said finally. "Just make sure you know who you aiming at before you pull the trigger."

He pulled his hood back up and turned toward the door.

"Apple…" Cash called.

Apple stopped, one hand on the door.

"Appreciate you slidin' through," Cash said. "I know what this is. But whatever happen next… stay sharp. Ain't no safety no more."

Apple nodded once. "Always." Then he disappeared into the rain.

Cash stood alone again, the hum of silence louder than before. He poured the last of the Hennessy into his glass and raised it slightly, like a toast to ghosts.

"If they want war," he muttered, "they gon' get it."

The rain hammered harder. Somewhere in the city, sirens started wailing—long, distant, like a warning. Cash didn't move. He just stared into the shadows, knowing the storm had already begun.

The faint beep of the heart monitor echoed through the sterile ICU room, breaking the silence every few seconds. K9 lay there, eyes half-open, his body weak, but his mind racing like a storm. Tubes ran into his arm, his chest rose and fell slowly, and every breath reminded him he was still alive—barely. The painkillers dulled the sting in his body, but not the questions burning through his mind.

He stared at the ceiling, replaying everything in his head. The streets were saying Cash sent them shooters, that this was all payback. But K9 couldn't buy that. *Nah... that don't sound right,* he thought to himself. He had just been with Cash not too long ago—broke bread with him, shared smoke, even talked plans about tightening up the money flow. Cash had plenty of chances to line him up right there if he wanted to. Ain't no reason to wait.

K9's jaw clenched as he remembered the flashes—the rain of bullets, the sound of glass shattering, the heat burning through his shoulder. He saw one of them shooters. The way he moved, the way he held that switch… he wasn't from Cash's circle. Cash's crew had a different rhythm, a different aim. Them boys wasn't his. Unless… unless Cash brought in some out-of-town hitters. But why would he? There wasn't no reason deep enough for Cash to cross him like that.

His mind drifted to Snake Eyes. The way Snake been moving lately—too calm, too quiet, too strategic. When word hit the streets about the shooting, Snake Eyes was the first to come stand next to him, claiming he had his back, claiming he was riding for him. But something about that didn't sit right. Snake Eyes was quick—too quick—to jump on his side, too eager to point fingers at Cash.

"Why now?" K9 whispered to himself, his voice raspy. "Why he so ready to ride, like he knew it was comin'?"

The monitor beeped a little faster as his thoughts sharpened. His instincts—the same ones that kept him alive all these years in the streets—were starting to flare. He'd been set up before, but never like this. This one felt personal. It felt like somebody wanted him to move reckless, to go at Cash without thinking.

He closed his eyes, breathing slow, letting the pain run through him. "Nah… this don't add up," he murmured. "Snake Eyes tryna play chess, but I see the board now."

Visions of the streets flickered in his mind—the corners, the faces, the alliances. Everything looked different now. He wasn't just fighting for survival; he was fighting to see the truth.

When he opened his eyes again, they were colder. Sharper.

If it was Cash, he thought, *I'll find out. But if it wasn't... then somebody close to me about to pay heavy.*

The machines kept beeping, but in K9's mind, the noise faded away. All he could hear was the rhythm of revenge building in his chest.

Chapter 12

The low hum of the air conditioner buzzed through the pool hall, blending with the clack of billiard balls and the faint echoes of old rap music coming from a Bluetooth speaker behind the bar. The neon "Open" sign flickered red and blue against the smoke-filled room. Mac Ru leaned against the green felt table, blunt tucked between his fingers, his gold chain glimmering faintly in the dim light. Savage stood across from him, lining up a shot, a glass of Henny half-empty beside the corner pocket.

They'd been out of town for a few days, laying low after the hit. Nobody knew where they were except a few trusted heads from their circle. The news about K9 being shot had already spread through New York like wildfire, and the talk on the streets was that Cash had called the hit—exactly the way Mac Ru planned it.

"Man, look at this," Mac Ru said with a smirk, exhaling a slow stream of smoke toward the ceiling. "Whole city think Cash did it. Boy can't even breathe right now. Every move he make, he gon' be lookin' over his shoulder."

Savage didn't even crack a smile. He missed the shot, the cue ball spinning off to the rail and stopping short. He slammed his cue down and grabbed his drink. "That ain't enough, Ru. Dude still breathin'. K9 supposed to be gone, not sittin' in some ICU fightin' for his life. You saw what that dude did to my family, how he killed her. Now he get to wake up and tell stories? While she fuckin' dead. Nah, I can't sleep right knowin' that."

Mac Ru chuckled, his tone calm, unbothered. "You always want everything done now, huh? You gotta learn patience, my boy. The best revenge ain't always fast—it's when they least expect it. We already got the streets twisted. K9 probably sittin' there thinkin' Cash did it too. Let 'em kill each other off while we watch from the sideline. That's how bosses move."

Savage shook his head, pacing around the table. "I hear you, Ru, but you know how this game go. If K9 get back on his feet, he ain't gon' stop till he find out who really touched him. He know faces, man. He not dumb. What if he remember seein' us?"

Mac Ru blew another cloud of smoke and watched it curl into the dim light. "He ain't see us. All he saw was flashes—dark car, tinted windows. I made sure of that. Besides, he had too much goin' on to even think straight. He was ridin' from Cash's block. The streets gon' line that up in they head and say, 'Yeah, Cash musta sent them hitters.' That's how rumors work—you just give 'em a spark, and they build the fire theyself."

He took a slow sip of his drink and leaned back on the table, eyes half-closed. "And now? Snake Eyes out there talkin' 'bout ridin' for K9. That boy already lining up to go at Cash and his crew. This whole thing gon' explode without us even shootin' another bullet."

Savage sighed, rubbing his jaw. "You too calm, bro. You forget who K9 was? That dude had pull everywhere—Queens, Harlem, BX, Brooklyn. You take a shot at him, even if it don't kill him, you light up the city. You think Cash gon' be the only one gettin' hit? Nah, they gon' start sniffin' around, connectin' dots. Word get out we was missin' right after the hit? People gon' talk."

Mac Ru smiled again, slow and cold. "Let 'em talk. Talk don't kill. Bullets do. And right now, the only people that can't talk are K9's driver and that second-in-command. You saw how we left it. That was art." He took another pull from his blunt. "Trust me, we ghosts. Nobody can put us at that scene. And while they tryna put it on Cash, we stackin' up, makin' our next move."

Savage took another shot at the table, this time sinking two balls in quick succession. His tone softened, but his eyes stayed sharp. "Man, I just don't like unfinished business. I been waitin' to line K9 up since that night he had our plug robbed. I wanted him gone, period. Now he still got breath in his lungs. That ain't sittin' right with me."

Mac Ru leaned forward, his voice low and deliberate. "And that's why I keep you close, Savage. You got that fire. But fire without control burn everything—even you. Let me handle the chessboard. I ain't gon' let K9 walk away from this. But for now, the best move is no move. Let Snake Eyes and Cash tear each other apart. When the smoke clear, we slide in, clean up whoever left, and take everything. That's how kings play this game."

Savage looked at him, thinking it over. The logic made sense, but the rage in his chest still burned too hot to cool down. He took another gulp of Henny and pointed his cue at Mac Ru. "Alright, Ru. I'm ridin' with you. But if that dude survive and start talkin', I'm finishin' it myself. You feel me?"

Mac Ru nodded slowly, flicking ash into the tray. "You got my word. If K9 make it out that hospital, he won't make it far. But till then, we chill. We ghosts, remember?"

A couple of locals walked in, laughing loud, throwing quarters on a nearby table. The bartender wiped glasses behind the counter, barely paying attention. The two hitmen looked like any other out-of-town hustlers, blending right into the backdrop.

Mac Ru walked over to the jukebox, dropped a few bills in, and played an old Nas track: "The World Is Yours." The beat filled the hall, steady and reflective. He stood there a second, head bobbing slightly, eyes cold. "That's the thing, Savage," he said over his shoulder. "They all out there fightin' for corners and respect. Me? I'm buildin' something that don't crumble when a bullet fly. Let them bleed while we build."

Savage chuckled for the first time that night. "You sound like you tryna be the mayor or somethin'."

"Nah," Mac Ru said, grinning as he chalked the cue. "I ain't no mayor. I'm the one the mayor call when he need something done."

He leaned over and sank the eight ball with a single smooth stroke. The ball dropped with a quiet thunk, and the room fell silent except for the hum of the AC. Mac Ru stood up straight, blew out a final puff of smoke, and said coolly, "Game over."

Savage stared at him, then cracked a smile and shook his head. "Yeah, alright, boss. Game over… for now."

They clinked their glasses together, the sound sharp and final, like a gunshot that echoed longer than the smoke it came from.

The bar smelled like stale beer and lemon cleaner. Neon from the sign outside cast a sickly red across the empty stools. Only one jukebox in the corner hummed on loan from better nights, playing a slow blues that swallowed the room. Cash stood at the head of the long, scarred bar, palms flat on the lacquered wood, sleeves rolled up. The light caught the gold on his knuckles; his face was a map of decisions he hadn't wanted to make.

Symone sat to his left, calm like a pool, watching everyone with a patient, tired stare. Big Apple leaned against the mirrored wall behind them, a cigar smoldering between his fingers, though there wasn't a soul to impress. Test occupied a cracked leather booth, fingers drumming a steady tattoo on the table. Around them—Norm, Rafe, Lil' D—faces that could settle accounts and start trouble in the same breath. No patrons, no prying ears. Cash had insisted on it that way.

"I said I wanted a quiet place," Cash said. His voice had a razor edge. "I asked for a plan, not chatter. This is family. This is serious."

Big Apple spat a curl of smoke toward the ashtray, listened, then nodded. "We ain't here to talk 'bout feelings. We here to do business. Snake Eyes got one too many moves. K9 got hit—ain't no accident. Streets talking, and some of that talk pointin' at Cash." He let that hang in the air, a loaded pause.

"Streets lie," Rafe muttered, but there was no conviction in it. His jaw flexed; he'd been hearing things too.

Cash straightened, eyes cutting to everyone like someone reading a ledger. "Snake Eyes tried to make it look like me put out the hit. Heard that? Frame me. Make me look like the one who had shots fired through K9's window." He said the words like the taste of poison. "That makes him dangerous—for me, for all of you. If people think I'd move on K9, there's no telling where the blowback goes."

Symone shifted forward. "You sure that's what happened? That's a heavy claim." Her tone was even—soft, but steel underneath. She'd seen Cash soften and snap before; she knew how to read the danger lines.

"I'm sure enough." Cash's hand curled into a fist on the bar. "I ain't taking no chances. If Snake Eyes wants war and he's playin' chess with dirty moves, we gonna go clean. Make it obvious." He looked at Big Apple. "Time to pop the bottle, man. Time to finish this."

Big Apple's grin was slow, predatory. "You want him dead? Or you want him scared? Sometimes a broken hand talk louder than a dead man." He flicked ash, thinking in angles. "But you want him gone, I can get at him. I know cats who'll make sure Snake Eyes disappear quick and quiet."

Test cut in, sharp and practical. "Quick and quiet got its perks, but it got downsides. Snake Eyes got people. You pull a hit on him, the whole city gon' feel it. We need to think what come after. You want bodies droppin'? Or you want leverage?" He rested his chin on his palm. "We ain't cleaning up fire that burn the whole block."

Norm snorted. "Leverage? You mean blackmail? We sit on him, wait? Snake Eyes ain't the waitin' type."

Symone's gaze roamed the room, cataloguing exits and echoes. "Option three," she said quietly. "Make him look like his own problem. Force him to expose himself. If we make him move, he show his hand. Then we decide. No unnecessary attention on us."

Cash's laugh was bitter. "That's what I thought too. But he already tried to make me look bad. And K9—K9 is bleeding in a hospital bed for real. I don't care who started it; someone's gotta answer. I ain't about to play coy while boys dyin'."

Big Apple tapped the bar with his knuckle. "We hit him where it hurt. Reputation, pockets, crew. Make his moves costly. But if you want to pull the trigger, we do it for you. I don't like playin' kingmaker, but I don't like snakes in my house either."

Rafe's voice was quieter now, the thought of retaliation weighing. "If we do this, there's gonna be more blood. You ask us to go to war, Cash. This ain't a backyard scuffle."

"You think I don't know that?" Cash's answer was a low growl. "I know. I'm just tired of bein' on the back foot. Snake Eyes trying to frame me makes it personal. He brought this to me."

Symone reached across and laid a pale hand over Cash's knuckles. The gesture was small, almost soft in the hard room. "We can make him pay without making you the marquee. Let Big Apple stir trouble that look like someone else's doing. Let Test handle the cut-off money, contacts, suppliers. Rafe and Norm handle the streets. If he move to retaliate, we trap him. It's controlled. It's surgical."

Chapter 13

Big Apple and Tes waited with the kind of practiced rhythm that comes from doing dangerous things often enough to learn how to breathe through them.

They parked two blocks away in a sedan scrubbed clean of life: no papers, no receipts, no scent, no trash that could testify later. Tes killed the engine. The car sat in the dark like it was asleep. Big Apple checked his Glock once, then again—calm, exact. He didn't fidget. Men who fidget are the ones who make mistakes.

"You see him?" Tes whispered, voice thin with adrenaline.

Big Apple's mouth pulled into something that wasn't a smile. "They out front like roaches. Snake Eyes always got a crew he trust." His eyes stayed on the building. "That backbone snap easy if you tug the right string."

Tes exhaled. "We tug, you break."

They moved like they belonged to the shadows. Two silhouettes slipping between dumpsters, keeping tight to the seam where concrete met dark. The warehouse yard opened up past a sagging back door and a chain-link fence, a lot full of rusted pickups and a food truck sitting dead like it had given up.

Up front, a cluster of men lounged and laughed—too loose, too comfortable. The kind of comfort that gets you killed.

Big Apple's breath stayed hollow and measured. "You got eyes?" he asked.

Tes scanned, slow and careful. “Two on the roof. Three on the side. One by the truck. Snake Eyes inside with two lieutenants.” He paused. “He don’t expect tonight. He think he got time.”

Big Apple’s expression tightened. “Good.” He let the word land. “Then tonight we take time from him.”

Two blocks up, Detective Cross watched from a rooftop perch wedged between an old antenna and a satellite dish. Rain misted the lens of his binoculars, turning the city into a smeared watercolor of light and threat.

Cross had been watching Snake Eyes for months—dossiers, informants, half-truths stacked into something that still wouldn’t hold up in court. But Cross wasn’t building a case anymore. He was building a conclusion.

He hadn’t expected Big Apple to move like this.

His instincts barked at him: stop it or study it. If he stepped in now, he could slow the blood. If he waited, he could learn the whole shape of it—names, patterns, who moved like a leader and who moved like a follower. Either choice had a price.

And Cross had already made too many choices that cost him everything.

Big Apple and Tes slipped into the yard, following the fence line. Big Apple climbed a ladder with quiet speed, crested the roof, and flattened into the dark like he’d been born up there. Tes stayed ground-level, settling where he could see the loading door without giving up his outline.

From the roofline, Big Apple could hear laughter below—careless, loud. Snake Eyes leaned near the truck like a man who believed the world owed him space. The kind of confidence that makes you sloppy.

Big Apple lifted a gloved hand.

Tes gave a small nod.

The first two shots were small, controlled—meant to disrupt, not announce. One of Snake Eyes’ men folded with a sharp, surprised sound. Another jerked sideways, clutching at himself like he didn't believe what had just happened.

Then the night broke open.

Gunfire shredded the air. Sparks jumped off metal. The food truck groaned as bullets kissed it. Men scattered, shouting over each other, trying to find angles that didn't exist. Tes' return fire snapped from the side, steady and disciplined, pinning bodies down and forcing eyes toward the wrong threat.

Big Apple moved along the roofline like an executioner clocking his steps. He didn't spray. He placed. Every shot carried a decision.

Below, Snake Eyes dove behind the truck and barked orders, voice hoarse with anger and disbelief. His men tried to regroup, tried to answer chaos with chaos, but the rhythm was wrong—too loud, too emotional. The yard became fragments: isolated bursts, bodies scrambling, smoke and dust turning the night metallic.

Cross watched the choreography through glass and rain.

He noted how Big Apple moved. How Tes covered. How Snake Eyes, even cornered, still tried to command the air like the air belonged to him.

Then Snake Eyes ran.

For a breath, it looked like he might make it—sprinting across gravel, feet fighting for purchase. He threw a laugh over his shoulder like a challenge, like he could out-run consequence.

Big Apple dropped from the roof and chased him without hesitation.

They broke into the gap between warehouses—a patch of scrub and dead grass where light never stayed long. Snake Eyes stumbled around a fallen crate, lunging forward like desperation could become speed.

Big Apple hit him like a slammed door.

He grabbed Snake Eyes by the collar and yanked him back, hard. The Glock came up, not to fire at first, but to speak in a language Snake Eyes understood. The first strike snapped Snake Eyes' head sideways. The second took balance. The third took pride.

"You picked the wrong night," Big Apple said, voice low enough to feel like a secret.

Snake Eyes spit blood and laughed anyway—raw, bitter. "So this it? Cash sent you?" His grin twitched. "*Forget Cash.* You came for me? Then do what you gotta do."

Big Apple's eyes didn't change. "You talk too much."

Another strike. Another. Snake Eyes' mouth split, his words turning thick and ugly, but still he tried to shape a story out of pain.

"You think killing me fix anything?" he forced out. "You think you can patch the city by cutting one man out?"

Big Apple steadied his grip. He raised the Glock.

Two shots, close and final.

Snake Eyes sagged into the weeds like the night had finally let him go.

For a moment, the world narrowed to breathing—Big Apple's, Tes'—and the far-off swell of sirens that sounded like they belonged to somebody else's life.

Tes sprinted in, chest heaving. He looked at Snake Eyes on the ground, then at Big Apple. "That it?" he asked, like he needed the words to make it real.

Big Apple wiped the Glock with a cloth, slow and exact, like ritual. "That's it."

They moved fast after that. Tes rifled Snake Eyes' pockets, snatched his wallet, checked for anything that could matter later. Big Apple scanned the darkness for headlights, for silhouettes, for the glint of a barrel.

They reached the sedan.

And then the car screamed.

A sudden hail of rounds hammered the rear panel. Glass spiderwebbed. Metal snapped and sang. Big Apple felt a hot bite in his arm, then another sting higher—shoulder—pain arriving late behind adrenaline.

Tes swore and punched the ignition. The sedan lurched forward, tires spitting gravel, fishtailing toward the street.

Cross stepped out from the shadows with a rifle braced and steady, rain slicking his sleeves. He wasn't there to celebrate. He wasn't there to be a hero.

He was there because waiting felt like dying.

He fired again—not for the kill, but to stop them. The sedan skidded, corrected, and tore into the night, wounded but moving.

Big Apple gripped his shoulder, jaw clenched so hard it felt like his teeth might crack. Blood slid down his sleeve in a dark ribbon.

Tes didn't look back. He didn't need to.

Cross walked into the field where Snake Eyes lay, rain darkening the weeds, turning the ground into a cold stain. He crouched, studying the dead man's face like he might find an answer inside it.

"I had my money on you," Cross murmured—not to Snake Eyes, not really, but to the idea of him. "Now you just a body."

He stood as sirens grew louder, the city waking up hungry.

People would talk by morning. Men would pick sides by noon. Cash would hear and move, whether he wanted to or not. Snake Eyes' crew would scatter or retaliate—either way, it would be ugly. Big Apple would carry this night in his shoulder and in his soul, and Tes would bury it under the next job like that's what tomorrow was for.

Cross turned away before the first cruiser could see him clearly. The rain kept falling, patient and mean, like the city was washing its hands.

And somewhere in the dark, war adjusted its aim.

Detective Cross turned and walked away through the mist and sour air. He had watched a man he once bet on die in a field. He had watched a gangster he'd hoped to hook and haul into the light put two rounds into a face until the body stopped arguing with the world. He had pulled a trigger in his own way, and the city would keep spinning like it always did.

As Cross receded into the night, the yard became a tableau: smoking fractures of glass, a truck abandoned like a witness, a body gone still. Somewhere down the block, a reporter's phone would light up with the first hungry calls. Someone would say escalation in the morning and mean it like a verdict. People on stoops would wake and talk in low tones. In barrooms and whispered corners where alliances were traded for a drink, the night's account would be written and rewritten until it lost the texture of truth.

Big Apple's sedan vanished, tires spitting broken city behind it. Tes prayed without words, knuckles bleached on the wheel. Big Apple pressed his wound and watched the streetlights blur as the car ate distance. For the first time in a long time, he felt an ache that wasn't just in his shoulder. Something deeper. The hollow that shows up when a man makes a choice and has to live with the shape it leaves behind.

The city kept its lights like nothing had changed. It kept the hum, the low roar, the small insanities that made nights like this possible. Cross kept his steps steady. He still had his money, which felt like a stupid, tiny thing to have in his pocket when the body of the night lay at his feet. But it was the stupid, tiny thing that had nudged him to move when he should've stayed still, and it would make him hesitate next time he had two choices that felt equally ruinous.

Far away, a siren approached and passed, indifferent. Dealers on corners counted their take. Men who survived lived to rearm, to swear, to plot. For now, the field was a silent ledger: Snake Eyes, dead. Big Apple, wounded and dangerous. Tes, breathing too loud behind the wheel. Detective Cross, walking away with money in his jacket and a new kind of history in his head.

The night had teeth. Tonight, it had bitten.

Chapter 14

The hospital room was quiet except for the hum of fluorescent lights and the slow, stubborn beep of the heart monitor. K9 lay back against stiff pillows, bandages wrapped tight around his chest and arm, his body aching with every shallow breath. The smell of antiseptic and plastic filled the air, but his mind was nowhere near the hospital.

The TV mounted on the wall flickered to life with the nightly news.

"Breaking overnight," the anchor said, crisp and calm. "Local gang leader known as Snake Eyes was killed late last night in what police are calling a targeted shooting. No suspects have been identified at this time."

K9's eyes locked on the screen. Flashing lights. Yellow tape. Shell casings scattered like punctuation. Then a still photo of Snake Eyes: that smirk, the diamond catching the light, the face that once ruled half the East Side. A caption ran across the bottom: notorious kingpin killed.

K9 didn't blink. His jaw tightened, and for a moment the pain in his chest wasn't the loudest thing in the room.

"Witnesses say a black SUV pulled alongside the victim's vehicle around midnight, opening fire with automatic weapons," the anchor continued. "Police recovered more than fifty shell casings at the scene. Officials are pursuing multiple leads, but no arrests have been made."

A nurse cracked the door to check the monitors. K9 waved her off without looking. He didn't want small talk. He wanted silence, because inside his head the noise was building.

He could see it now. The rhythm. The way the board was being cleaned.

First he got hit leaving Cash's block, an ambush so clean it almost felt rehearsed. Now Snake Eyes was gone less than a week later. Two major moves, too close together, too precise to be random.

He'd been trying to convince himself Cash didn't have anything to do with his shooting. Cash had opportunity and didn't take it. Cash had been right there, close enough to end him with a word, and he hadn't.

But this? Snake Eyes dead right after Cash's name had been dragged through the streets?

K9 stared at the frozen face on the screen.

"This what it is now?" he muttered. "This how you moving, Cash?"

Anger rose through him, slow and poisonous, pulsing harder than the IV drip. The streets were already talking: Cash set up K9. Snake Eyes sided with K9 out of guilt or fear. Now that Snake Eyes was dead, those whispers wore the shape of truth.

The broadcast shifted to a detective at a press conference. "We believe the shooting was planned," the detective said. "This was not random. We're urging anyone with information to come forward."

K9 gave a dry, bitter sound. "Ain't nobody coming forward," he said to nobody. "Not where we from."

He reached for the phone beside the bed, grimacing as a sharp pain cut through his ribs. He dialed from muscle memory. Two rings, then a familiar voice.

"Yo, it's Manny."

"You see the news?" K9 asked.

"I'm watching it now," Manny said. "They talking like it's a war about to start."

"It already started," K9 replied, voice rough but steady. "Cash did this. I know it."

Manny hesitated. "You sure, boss? You was just with him before you got hit. He looked shook. Maybe somebody else—"

"Don't finish that," K9 snapped. "Ain't no maybe. You think Snake Eyes just end up dead the week after I get lit up? Come on. Cash trying to clean the board. He knew Snake Eyes was standing with me. Now he gone. You see what that mean?"

Manny went quiet. Traffic hissed faint in the background.

"Boss," he said finally, "you want me to move?"

"Not yet," K9 said, rubbing his temple with two fingers. His eyes drifted back to the TV footage: the black SUV, the chaos, the clean getaway. "I need information. Find out who Snake Eyes met with yesterday. Who he called. Who he rode with. And I want somebody watching Cash's warehouse. Every car in and out. Plates. Faces. Anything."

"Copy," Manny said. "You think he'll move again?"

"I know he will," K9 murmured. "Cash don't make noise unless he got a reason. But he slipped. This too neat. You don't erase a man like Snake Eyes without somebody noticing. And I noticed."

"What you want me to do if I catch something solid?"

"Bring it straight to me," K9 said. "No moves until I say so. I want to look him in the face before anything happens. I want him to see me. Not a rumor. Not a ghost. Me."

He coughed, pain biting. He took a slow breath.

"And Manny."

"Yeah, boss?"

"Tell the crew tighten up. No loose talk. We move quiet, but we watching everything. Cash think I'm laid up and out the game… let him believe that." K9's voice dropped. "But I'm coming."

"You got it," Manny said. "I'll call you soon."

K9 ended the call and stared at the TV again. Snake Eyes' face sat there mid-smile, like he was mocking him from the other side.

K9 switched the TV off and closed his eyes. The hum of the lights filled the room, but in his head the streets were already awake, and every step from here on out would be war.

Big Apple limped into Cash's spot like a man who'd spent the night walking through lightning and somehow lived. His jacket hung open at the shoulder, bandage peeking beneath the collar. A cigarette sat in the corner of his mouth, burning down to the filter. His jaw was set in that crooked way Cash recognized: steady even when he was bleeding.

Cash looked up from behind the bar and let out a breath that was half laugh, half relief. He didn't rush in front of his people, but the room shifted anyway. The crew gathered like gravity had changed.

"You look like hell," Cash said low.

Big Apple pulled the cigarette out, spoke like it was nothing. "Did what had to be done. Snake Eyes ain't walking the earth no more."

Cash let the words sit. Then he gave a short laugh, the kind that sounded almost brotherly. "I knew I could trust you with that."

He slapped Big Apple's good shoulder and Big Apple didn't flinch, just exhaled and took the seat. One of Cash's people cleaned the wound in silence. A woman in the corner poured shots slow. For a few minutes they joked—old stories, bitter laughs, the kind of warmth men borrow from the past to survive the present.

When the laughter faded, Big Apple looked at Cash like he was weighing him, cataloging him.

"You know I love you," Big Apple said, sudden and plain. "You my brother for life."

Cash's chest tightened, but his voice stayed even. "Likewise. I love you more."

Big Apple nodded once, a rare softness in the gesture. Then he pushed up, slid toward the door, and disappeared into the wet night.

Outside, the street smelled like rain and old coffee. Big Apple got into his car with a stiff grace, started the engine, and drove until the city noise thinned into something quieter, something personal. When he pulled up across from his block, he killed the engine and opened the door.

A movement cut the shadows.

Detective Cross stepped out like a thought made solid. Hood up. Face tight. Eyes empty in that way grief makes them when it's been sharpened into purpose.

Cross didn't shout. He didn't warn. He moved fast, closed distance, and drove the butt of his pistol into the side of Big Apple's head.

Big Apple hit the pavement hard, the world flashing white for a second. He tried to push up, but Cross was already there, crouched close, voice low and cold.

"You killed my wife," Cross said. "You killed my child. You burned my house. You think you get to sleep in peace?"

The words were measured, memorized. Not a rant. A sentence being read.

Big Apple turned his head and laughed once, ugly and short. He spit blood and venom in the same breath. "Forget your wife and kid. Do what you gonna do."

Cross's face didn't change. His hands tightened. The pistol was steady, not shaking, not angry. Just certain.

"You don't get to say that," Cross said.

Big Apple tried to rise, tried to pull the world back under him, but he was half a second behind the decision already made.

Cross fired.

The shots were quick. Controlled. Not a performance. A conclusion.

Big Apple folded back to the pavement, breath leaking out of him like the city had finally taken its receipt. His eyes found Cross's face, and for a flicker there was something like respect in them, mixed with acceptance, like he'd known this was one of the endings his life had earned.

He moved his mouth, voice barely there.

"Tell Cash… I did what I had to."

Detective Cross watched him as if he expected, perversely, him to come back up and laugh at him. When he didn't, some of the hardness seeped from him, replaced by a hollow that had nothing to do with the law. He stood, put her hoodie up like armor, and walked away. There was no satisfaction in it that sang; it was a completion, an ending, a box closed on a chapter he'd been forced to write in blood and smoke.

By dawn, the news vans were there like vultures with microphones. Cameras were arrayed in a mess, anchors' faces breaking open into that practiced expression television gives to death when it equals spectacle. Flashbulbs punctured the gray. Reporters circled, faces smooth with the kind of righteous curiosity that televises grief. "Breaking: local gang member killed outside his home," they said. The segment rolled on like a wheel; the image on the screen was Big Apple slumped across the pavement, the light from the streetlamp catching the angles of his fall. The voiceover said words that mattered less than the picture: suspected ties, ongoing investigations, community outrage.

Cash stood in his living room with the television's light painting his face in cold hues. He had been at the bar the night before, a drink balancing his hands and the world feeling like something he could weigh and shape. Now every line in his chest felt carved by a new grief. His hands twitched once, twice, and the room around him seemed to thin until it was nothing but the humming box and the image of his brother.

The blunt he'd been saving for a later celebration burned in an ashtray, untouched. He watched, eyes narrowed not with the burning need to retaliate but with the sudden, incredulous grief of someone who had lost a part of himself to the street he'd helped build. "No," he muttered at the screen, though no one could hear him. The word was both denial and a rebellion.

For a moment, he let the scene unfold in his head differently. He saw Big Apple alive, leaning on the hood of his car, taking one last drag, smiling at a joke no one else heard. He saw him stumbling into the light of Cash's respect and loyalty, proud in a peculiar, stubborn way. He remembered the hurt that had scarred Big Apple's face, the way he steadied his crew when things went sideways. He remembered the laugh, the half-sob, the big shoulders that had carried more than their weight.

Then reality reasserted itself with the low glare of the television: detectives on the scene, evidence tape, a silhouette of a woman with a hood walking away. Cash folded his hands until the knuckles whitened. The sound of his heart was loud in his ears, a drumbeat that kept time with a procession of choices he had not yet made.

He could have called his crew. He could have burned the block to the ground. He could have answered violence with violence and wrapped his entire world in the same taste of ash and retribution. Instead, he stood very still, as if the stillness itself might keep him from doing something he could never take back. He felt, for the first time in a long time, the real weight of consequence settle on him—not as an abstraction, but as a physical thing that pulled at his stomach.

Big Apple, lying on the pavement, had not been a simple nigga. His life had been full of choices, some cruel, some born from hate, some made in the cold light of survival. Detective Cross knew that he had killed people she loved, but the act of killing him had not lifted the smell of smoke from her memories, nor returned the warmth to the arms of those she had lost. She walked home with a hollow that was neither triumph nor peace.

She did not call it justice. She called it a closure no courtroom had offered her. Later, when the reporters asked, when her superiors probed and prodded and catalogued, she would tell the sanitized version: opportunity, immediate threat, homicide. But for now, in the quiet that followed, she felt only the rawness of her grief and the numbness of an act that could not be taken back.

Cash watched the footage again, slower, as if rewinding might let him see the moment he could have changed. He saw Big Apple's face, calm and unafraid. He saw the man in the hoodie, small, walking away as if she had finally laid a ghost to rest. The image dug under his ribs like a cold knife. He wanted to believe Big Apple had not been scared. He needed to believe it. So he let the belief mask the rest: the guilt, the betrayal woven through their world, the fact that the woman whose hands had pulled the trigger on another man's life had walked away and would sleep tonight.

By afternoon, the street had a new story to tell. People gathered on stoops, mouths moving in the half-speech of rumor. Some cried out for vengeance. Others said that this was a cleansing, that big names do not fall without ripples. Cash's crew gathered in the back room of the bar, faces drawn, voices low. A younger kid in the corner clenched his fists like a child trying to hide a bruise. The room smelled of cigarette smoke and diesel and the kind of fear that comes from knowing, largely, what will happen next.

Cash shut the back-room door and looked at the men who had always been close enough to be family and far enough to be untouchable. He watched their eyes. He watched their shoulders. Then he watched the mirror behind the bar, which reflected his own face—the face of a man who had built his empire on the edges of law and loyalty and now had to decide whether more of the same could save him.

He thought of Big Apple's last glance, the easy way he had said, "I love you," and the even easier way he had said, "Likewise." Those words had weight now. They were not just words; they were a ledger, a promise. Cash felt the promise in his throat like a lump he could not swallow. He realized then that loyalty was not a business term; it was a currency that, once spent, could not be reclaimed.

Detective Cross, at the same time, sat in a car a block away from the bar, hands on the steering wheel, replaying the exact sequence of events in her head like someone who had rehearsed the lines and still felt as if she'd forgotten a cue. She had done what she'd set out to do, and the reality of it pressed against her sternum. Satisfaction? Maybe. Relief? Not really. She had wanted, for so long, to stop this man, to stop the ledger of deaths and the hollowed-out lives he left in his wake. Now it was done, and there was nothing to fill the hollow bay where her family had been.

The television in Cash's living room rolled into the night, spitting out talking heads who skimmed the edges of truth and fed the public's appetite for drama. Analysts speculated about gang retaliation, about the dent this would make in the local balance of power. The city held its breath, waiting for the next chapter. In the hush between one news cycle and the next, real people made real choices.

For a night, for a narrow, fragile hour, Cash allowed himself to feel the rawness of being human. He drank a glass of something that burned like old guilt and sat at the window watching the city—the same city he had carved his corners from—move on. He thought of Big Apple's face, the way it had folded in the light, the small, proud smile. He thought of the vows that had been traded in a room that smelled of smoke and cheap liquor. "You my brother for life," Big Apple had said. Cash said it back in his head and meant it in a way that now counted for nothing but memory.

He didn't sleep that night. He walked the house like a man with nothing to do but measure loss. Somewhere in the back of his mind, a plan began to percolate—not one of immediate blood for blood, but of strategy. He would not let the world he'd built unravel into chaos. That was not the same as forgiveness. It was survival.

Detective Cross, meanwhile, went home and sat with a pile of photographs and notes and legal forms, the paper equivalent of the life she'd been trying to rebuild. She lit a cigarette and felt something like a tremor of guilt flutter through her chest, but she stacked it away with the rest of the paperwork. The law had a way of blurring when the heart wanted clarity.

The next morning, the city buzzed anew. People whispered that a war might begin. Some prayed for it, some dreaded it. But regardless of what the street wanted, what happened was already in motion: a man had been taken out in a single, decisive act, and there would be consequences that could not be contained to a single headline.

Big Apple's funeral—because there would be one, as there is for every legend and loss—would be a mirror of the life he'd led: mournful, brazen, full of show and sorrow. Cash would stand at the front and feel, in a way that was hard and carved, the emptiness grow. Detective Cross would watch from a distance and wonder whether the justice she had claimed was honest or just another shade. The city would whisper that retribution was coming, like a shadow stretched long by a low sun.

And in the quiet places where people live and breathe and try to find meaning, those who remained would have to learn how to carry on with the knowledge that one person's choice had tilted the world just a little. They would have to decide whether to let the tilt become a tumble or to brace and rebuild.

For Cash, for Detective Cross, for the crew, and for the city, the night had rearranged the pieces of a game played on a street that never truly forgave. The next move belonged to those who had the muscle to make it. For now, they had a body on the pavement and a name on the news, and the taste of something bitter and final on their tongues.

Big Apple had died with a laugh and a half-sentence of instructions. Detective Cross had walked away with her hands still shaking. Cash had been left to reckon with the fact that the man he loved as a brother had died in a way that was small and big all at once. The world spun on, and under the city lights, the war that had once been a rumor now had a face.

Chapter 15

Cash smoked a blunt. He looked at the photo on the desk—him, Apple, and Tes after their first big score years ago. Smiles, bottles, loyalty before the money and the blood.

Before he could even sit back down, his phone rang again. This time, the name on the screen froze him completely.

K9.

Cash stared at the screen for a few seconds, confusion mixing with rage. K9 never called unless it was serious, and after everything that went down—the rumors, the shootouts, the tension—this call meant something.

He pressed accept.

"What?" Cash said coldly.

K9's voice was calm, steady—too calm. "I heard about your man, Big Apple. I know y'all was tight. My condolences, bro."

Cash said nothing, his jaw locked. He could hear the hum of a ceiling fan on K9's end, maybe some music faint in the background.

"I need you to come see me," K9 continued. "At my house. It's time we talk man-to-man. This can't keep goin' like this. Too much blood already hit these streets."

Cash let the silence stretch. He could feel every muscle in his face tighten.

"I'll be there," he said finally, grinding his teeth so hard the words came out sharp.

Then he hung up.

He grabbed his jacket, his gun, and his keys. Tes tried to stop him at the door.

"Yo, you sure that's smart, Cash? You don't even know if this a setup."

Cash cut him off. "If K9 wanted me dead, I'd already be gone. This ain't that. This… this somethin' else."

He got in his black SUV, engine growling as he pulled out into the night. The rain had just started, smearing the city lights into red and gold streaks across the windshield. Every mile he drove, he replayed memories—him and Big Apple posted up on the block, laughing about how they'd make it out the game one day. Now his man was gone, and all Cash had left was anger and ghosts.

When he finally turned down K9's block, there were no guards out front like usual. Just two black SUVs parked with tinted windows and one porch light glowing. Cash's instincts were on full alert.

He parked across the street, slipped his hand under his hoodie, and walked up the driveway. The door opened before he could knock.

K9 stood there, one arm still bandaged from the hospital, wearing a dark hoodie and sweatpants. His face was unreadable—not anger, not sadness. Just cold focus.

"Come in," K9 said quietly.

Cash stepped inside. The house was quiet, almost too quiet. A half-empty bottle of Hennessy sat on the table, two glasses beside it.

"Sit down, bro," K9 said, pouring a drink.

Cash didn't move for a moment, then finally sat across from him, eyes locked.

K9 slid a glass his way. "To the fallen," he said.

Cash stared at the drink but didn't touch it. "You said you wanted to talk. So talk."

K9 took a sip, leaned back, and sighed. "This war between us? It's done. It stops tonight. I ain't call you here to argue, and I damn sure ain't call you to set you up. Too many people dead already. Too much money lost. Too much heat on both sides."

Cash said nothing, but his fingers tapped the table, restless.

"I know you hurtin' about Big Apple," K9 continued. "He was loyal. But you gotta see what's goin' on, man. These streets don't care who started it anymore. It's just kill or be killed. You and Snake Eyes both—Snake Eyes is dead. Y'all both losin' family."

Cash's jaw flexed. "You talkin' like you ain't part of this, K9. Like your Snake Eyes ain't been shootin' at mine. You forget who lit the match?"

K9's eyes narrowed. "Don't do that. You know damn well I ain't have nothin' to do with Snake Eyes or that hit on Apple. I ain't blind, Cash. Somebody else playin' both sides, keepin' this war alive while we kill each other."

Cash leaned forward, voice sharp. "You expect me to believe that after what I seen? After the rumors, after the drive-bys?"

K9 slammed his drink down, eyes burning now. "You believe what you want. But look around. Snake Eyes gone. Big Apple gone. Who's next? You? Me? You really think that's worth it?"

The room fell silent. The rain outside tapped against the window, steady and cold.

Cash finally reached for the glass, staring into the dark liquor. His reflection rippled in it like a broken mirror.

"I buried too many already," he said softly. "But Big Apple… he was different. That one hit my soul."

K9 nodded slowly. "I know that pain. I felt it too. That's why I'm sayin' this stops now. No more blood on the streets. We got bigger things to worry about. Cops watchin' every move. Feds buildin' cases. If we keep goin', we both end up in a cell or a grave."

Cash looked up, studying him. He saw something in K9's eyes—not weakness, but exhaustion. The kind of weariness that comes from years of losing people you love to a game that never gives back.

After a long silence, Cash nodded once.

"Alright."

K9 looked surprised. "Alright?"

"Yeah," Cash said. "You right. This ends tonight. For Apple. But fuck Snake Eyes—and for all the ones we lost."

He stood up and extended his hand. K9 looked at it for a second, then took it. The shake was firm—old enemies, old friends, bound by pain.

Cash turned to leave but stopped at the door. "Just know this, K9: if somebody break this peace, I ain't holdin' back next time."

K9 nodded. "Neither will I."

As Cash stepped back into the rain, thunder rolled overhead. For the first time in weeks, the city felt quiet—too quiet. He looked up at the dark clouds and whispered under his breath,

"Rest easy, Apple. It's over now… at least for tonight."

He got back in the SUV, the engine rumbling low as he pulled away. Behind him, K9 stood in the doorway, watching the taillights disappear. He poured the last of his drink out on the porch, a silent tribute to the ones who didn't make it.

The streets had gone silent. But both men knew that peace in this world never lasted long.

***

The church smelled like lilies and diesel—lilies from the floral arrangements piled high by the casket, diesel from idling cars packed tight outside. Men in suits that had seen better days stood shoulder to shoulder with kids in hoodies and old women who clutched rosaries like lifelines. Someone had brought a boombox; a slow R&B song—Brandy's *Missing You*—crawled through the speakers and tried to hold the room together.

Big Apple lay in a polished mahogany casket like a man who'd been dressed up for someone else's idea of peace. His hair was perfect, his face arranged into the softest version of the man who had been sharp, loud, dangerous on the block. People leaned over the rails and whispered his name like a prayer or an accusation, depending on who was listening. The pews were full; the back of the church spilled into the courtyard, where others stood with their hands in their pockets, watching.

Cash sat in the third row from the front. He didn't cry. He didn't need to. He sat with a kind of stillness that was a different animal—a quiet that felt like a storm funneling in his chest. Beside him, Tes kept his hat low, shoulders tight as if they could hold the world up. Around them were faces from the old days and the new; faces that had counted on Big Apple, that had trusted him with their lives. Now those faces were hollow in places only grief and calculation could reach.

Every so often someone would stand to speak—a cousin, a preacher, an old friend who talked about Apple's laugh and how he'd hold his ground for anybody who needed him. They told stories of his loyalty and the way he'd cover a man's back without asking why. People wiped their eyes. A kid said, "He was my uncle," and half the room sobbed like a river had been cut loose.

Detective Cross walked in quietly, wearing a coat too light for the weather and an expression that didn't fit the place. The murmurs hummed higher as heads turned. There were cops at the perimeter—cruisers double-parked down the block and uniformed officers standing like silent sentries on the curb. They had badges, clipboards, radios clipped at their hips. Everyone noticed them, cataloged them; but this was a funeral. Even somebody who carried a badge had to move through the grief without making a bigger wave than the rest.

Cross moved up the center aisle slow, like he was trying to keep his steps from making noise. He stopped at the casket, placed one gloved hand on the varnished wood, and reached into his inside coat pocket. He drew out a single rose, cradled it like a confidential file, and lowered it gently onto Apple's chest. The flower was the only bright thing in the room for a second.

Every eye in the place found him. For a breathless moment, the world contracted—the minister paused mid-sentence, someone's child began to cry. Cross looked up just long enough to meet Cash's gaze. There was a hardness in his face that the sunlight couldn't soften. He turned and walked out without a word, the rose left like a mute accusation.

Cash watched him go. People followed Cross with their eyes like he was a comet passing through their private sky. For those who knew what to read, there was something in Cross's posture that didn't belong at a funeral: the shoulders that didn't slump, the jaw that didn't tremble, the movement of a man carrying information and deciding how to store it.

After the service, there were handshakes. People hugged. Someone lit a cigar by the curb. A couple of men argued in low voices about who'd take care of what; a woman broke down so hard her sister had to hold her up. Cash stood apart. He let the line of mourners pass. He listened to the eulogies on autopilot, filed the names, the promises. He let the smell of lilies and smoke and diesel soak into his clothes like a memory you can't scrub out.

K9 was there, too—bandaged arm wrapped tight, hat pulled low. He moved through the crowd like someone trying to keep his wounded body from announcing his presence. He gave Cash a look that said the same thing they'd both been thinking: this had gone too far. But both of them, standing in the doorway of the church, knew that words could be bargains only when the fingers that signed them were clean. Their fingers were not clean.

Detective Cross left through the side door. Cash watched until his silhouette blended with the streetlamps and then darted into the waiting crowd. He had a plan, the shape of it like a blade in his hand. He let it sit there; funerals were for promises, and action was for after.

They moved like water around each other afterward. Tes and two others—quiet faces that had been with Cash since before the big moves—disappeared into a back room with a laptop that had a stubborn fan and a hunger for evidence. Cash didn't sleep. He watched the footage as if he'd find Apple's breath still in it, some error that would say the whole thing was a bad dream.

The surveillance camera had been cheap and mounted high, the kind that caught more sky than faces. But when they spooled the night of the hit, it fed the truth in small, grainy pieces.

A shadow. A whisper of motion. A pair of shoes. A figure moving past the porch light like a goddamn phantom. Big Apple stepping out, looking to the left, then the right. A hand—careful, not frantic—pulling something from under a coat. The frame jittered with interference, then froze long enough for Tes to say, "Pause."

Cash leaned in. The figure moved closer. The camera angle shifted, and then, in a moment that should not have fit the world, Cross stepped forward, his coat collar up like a man trying to hide. He was close. Too close. Big Apple didn't have time to turn. The sound on the video was a hiss of static and the clack of shoes. There was a flash at eye level—a white bloom on the feed—and then Apple folded like a curtain.

Cash didn't feel anything for a beat. Then something hot and sharp woke up in him. He hit play again. Cross lifted the gun. He leaned in, and the little camera, indifferent, recorded the act the way a stone records ripples. Cross put the gun back in his coat and walked off camera with the matter-of-factness of a man taking his evening walk. The frame ended on Apple's stillness.

"Play that back," Cash said, and when they did it again, the room had a different smell. Tes swore under his breath.

The others' faces turned papery and small. K9 slapped the table, a sound like someone trying to keep their heart from jumping out.

Cash's hands had been steady all his life; now they weren't. He sat very still, and then he stood, and the world threaded itself into something with a single direction. There was no argument to be had; there was only the ledger of what had been done and a cold, exacting need to balance it.

"You all right?" Tes asked, but Cash didn't answer. They'd all seen the video. They all felt the way the ground shifted under their feet.

"You know what to do," Cash said at last, his voice low as a confession. "We get the body. We don't let this sit in a morgue so the police can pin it on the wrong people. We take what's ours. We make sure the city knows there's a cost."

Chapter 16

Detective Cross never thought he was a man to be cornered. He drove a government-issue car because it kept him visible in a way armor does; he liked the recognition, the little godly protection it lent him. That night, his windshield fogged and a streetlight hummed. He had his badge on the dash, the simplicity of it like a last, honest gesture.

He was not expecting the SUV that came out of nowhere.

The first thing to go was momentum. The other car—black, heavy, like a moving slab of purpose—came across the intersection and hit him head-on. The world folded into a noise. Airbags burst like silent alarms. Metal moaned and glass shivered. Cross's head snapped forward and then slid back into the wheel. For a second he was weightless, like a puppet whose strings had been cut.

Cash emerged from the passenger door with the quiet of a shadow. He moved around the crumpled driver's side and looked at Cross, whose eyes were blinking with pain. Cross's head lolled, his mouth making small movements as he tried to chart what had happened.

"You slimy piece of—" Cash muttered, but it was a whisper meant for himself. The world had narrowed to the rhythm of his breath and the gun warming in his hand.

Cross's hand fumbled for the steering wheel, then for the glove compartment, then stopped. His mouth made a sound—maybe an apology, maybe a prayer. He didn't have the composure for a confession; he had only the flinch of a trapped animal.

"You expect me to ask you why?" Cash said, voice even. The rain had started again, a skeletal mist that blurred the streetlights. Cross's forehead was split, a film of blood in his hairline. His uniform was a crumpled map.

"I—" Cross tried. There was fear now, and something like a brittle calculation. His hand rose, maybe for a weapon he didn't have time to finish finding.

Cash didn't hesitate. He'd watched the footage a dozen times, and in each replay he'd felt the same cold mathematics lay down inside him: betrayal demanded ledger and action. He fired.

The sound broke the mist like a handclap. Cross jerked, a small, defiant reaction that had nowhere to land. The first round hit him square in the face. He didn't go into a graphic end; he simply slumped, the reality brutal in its finality, not ornamental in detail.

Cash's body moved like steel with purpose. He fired twice more. The shots were executions, professional and hollowed-out. When it was done, Cross's body was no longer a man waiting to be interrogated; he was a quiet thing, heavy and still against the steering column.

For a heartbeat, Cash looked at the motionless form as if the thing in the car might still be useful—information, leverage, testimony. He looked at the people in his crew, their eyes wide and hard at once. Tes swallowed and stepped closer, then knelt to check Cross's pulse. He shook his head.

"Get his body," Cash said. It was an order made of necessity and ritual. "Bring him with us. We ain't lettin' the cops parade this like some moral."

They worked with a speed that comes from long practice. Two men pried the door; another lifted Cross's limp weight into the back of the SUV. They moved like a team whose choreography had been calibrated by violence. None of them spoke. In the rearview, Cash watched Cross's face for the last time—the man who had walked in at a funeral and laid a rose on the dead and then, in secret, had become the hand that killed.

They loaded the body into the back and locked the doors. Cash sat behind the wheel and started the engine. The SUV pulled away into the rain. The city lights blurred into a ribbon of regret, and for once Cash didn't feel the blood-heat thrill of power. He felt the weight of a ledger closed with a slam that echoed in his ribs.

They drove away from the place where Cross's car still smoked in the intersection. They drove as if every light was a guard, every cop a judge. No one celebrated. No one cracked a smile. The men in the SUV thought of a thousand things—of the funeral hymn that had been half-sung, of Apple's laugh, of the crib where he'd slept as a kid, the first time he'd ever seen a shine of money and believed it could be theirs for good.

Cash kept the video playing in his head. He rewound it not to see the violence again but to find the moment the world had tipped. He needed a landmark. He needed a place to lay the blame so it would stop bleeding through the lives of the men who were left.

K9 sat across from Cash in the front seat, bandage a white stripe against his dark skin. He watched the road with the kind of attention that meant he was filing each second into a memory safe. The wound in his arm still ached; his hands had trembled in the church, and now they were steady.

"What now?" Tes asked quietly from the back.

Cash's hands tightened on the wheel. "Now we move like we didn't do it," he said. "We move like it never happened. We make sure people know Cross did it. We make sure the right names get attached to the right truths so nobody tries to pin this on us. We close ranks. We keep Apple's name clean. We keep our people from gettin' boxed in."

No one argued. They sat with the particulars of their lives and the knowledge that their choices would make waves they couldn't predict.

They turned the keys into different hands, sent men to arrange the next moves. Money changed hands to fix stories, to buy quiet, to put pressure on certain precincts with unspoken threats. Cash sat at the table in the warehouse as the city woke and tried to stitch itself back together. He thought about how a rose had once been a sign of honor and how now it meant a very different thing.

A rumor would spread, and in the world they moved in, rumors were often cheaper and harsher than facts. Some would say Cross had been shot by retribution. Some would say Cross had been killed by rival police in a dark exchange. Some would say Big Apple had been killed by men in hoods. The truth sat with Cash and his crew in a black SUV, in the dark, in the back of a truck heading down a highway with two hands heavier than they had been forty-eight hours before.

Cash knew what the consequence chain looked like: the police would ask questions. Friends would pick sides. Someone else would see the opening and try to take advantage. The balance of power would shift because blood has a way of making room for a new order.

He thought of Big Apple's laugh one last time—loud, patient, full of the cheap joy of a man who'd found a brother in the wrong place. He thought of the casket, of the rose, of Cross's gloves. And he thought of the city outside—not asleep, not dead, just waiting.

At the edge of the warehouse, a young boy from the block knocked on the door, eyes wide. He'd heard things and wanted to know who'd been left standing. Cash opened the door, and the kid looked up like somebody waiting for a hero or a warning.

"We bury him right," Cash said, and the boy nodded—not understanding the politics, but understanding the weight in the man's voice.

They would bury Big Apple. They would make sure he had a name on a stone and a story that fit the life he'd lived.

After that, they would move. Strategy would be spoken in tight tones. Threats would be made and perhaps met. But for one small, brittle day, the men in that dim warehouse allowed themselves to feel the emptiness and the cold—to mourn and to plan like the two acts of the same long, awful play.

Cash walked to the back of the warehouse and looked at the murals of the block painted years ago by some kid with too much talent and not enough permission. Big Apple's face was not on any wall; it would never be painted. But in Cash's head, he kept the sound of his laugh, the click of his boot on the pavement. He kept the way Apple had once slapped his shoulder hard in celebration. He kept the ledger and the violence and the quiet promise that justice would be paid.

Outside, the city moved on. Inside, they reloaded. The price was paid, but that didn't mean the debt was settled. The streets had a long memory. So did Cash.

***

They parked two blocks away and walked the rest, boots crunching on gravel, jackets zipped up against the cold that had nothing to do with the weather. The cemetery smelled like damp earth and old prayers, the kind of place the city sent people when it needed to keep them quiet in rows. The sky was a flat gray that made every dark thing look darker.

Big Apple's plot had been kept warm by flowers and a folded flag someone had left. Fresh dirt still clung to the edges of the mound like a bruise. Cash moved like he had rehearsed this a thousand different ways in a room with no windows. He carried the weight of the night in his shoulders, but he didn't breathe like a man who'd been hollowed out; he breathed like a machine that had been wound to an end and was now letting off steam.

They stopped a few paces back. K9 had the body wrapped in a tarp, the edges tied tight so there was no face to read and no blood to spill across someone's shoes. Tes and two others crouched down; their breaths came in little fogs, white and sharp. None of them spoke. Words felt like debris when the work was this particular.

Cash looked at the open grave beside Big Apple's, a shallow, ugly cut in the earth waiting to take another thing out of the world. The men who'd dug it had used muscle and hands and the clumsy sympathy that comes with hired labor—the hole left too close, too deliberate, as if whoever ordered it wanted it to be obvious. The smell of clay rose up, damp and honest.

"Put him down," Cash said, voice steady. Everyone obeyed.

They eased the tarp off enough to get handles on the body without looking at the face, the way you avoid a mirror in a room you used to love. The corpse was heavy and awkward, a human thing rearranged into a weight. Cash's men moved like men who'd done this before: coordinated, efficient, the tenderness of their motions submerged by routine.

When they reached the edge of the grave, Cash stepped forward, looking down. He let the tarp fall away in a slow, deliberate motion so the world could see what he wanted it to see. Detective Cross lay there, pale and still, the aggression of his life finally disarmed by the silence of death. The wounds were there—someone who knew how to make a face unreadable had already done that—but the important part was what the body had been: a man who had been allowed to hold the law's badge and then used that badge to pull a string that killed a brother.

Cash's hand hovered over the lip of the hole for a moment. The other men watched him as if he were a barometer, waiting for a sign to tell them which way the wind would blow next. Cash didn't let them be the judge and jury of him; he did what men do when pain hardens into ritual.

He nodded once, and they lowered Cross into the ground.

The body slipped into the dark with a small, decisive sound—the kind an old door makes when it's finally shut for good. Dirt began to fall in handfuls, the sound dry and intimate. At first it was just a rhythm: scoop, drop, tamp. Their shovels dug into wet earth, and skin-callused hands worked with the quiet fury born from watching too many people you loved go to sleep too soon.

Cash watched the soil cover Cross like he was watching a page being turned. He didn't speak. He didn't pray. He didn't look away. The men around him moved with the mechanical care of people following the rules of a game they'd learned from losses: cover the thing, erase the trail, make the ledger balance. Each handful of dirt made the shape in the grave smaller and more final.

When the last of the soil hit the body, Cash stepped forward and placed his boot on the edge of the fresh mound. He let his weight rest there like a punctuation mark. The cemetery held its breath, and the city outside kept spinning, and no one called the moment divine.

Cash looked at the men who had done the work with him: Tes, shoulders tight, jaw clenched; K9, bandage catching the dirt like a white flag with stains; the others, faces full of an exhausted blankness. He looked at them as if they were beneath his gaze already, as if they were the dirt covering Cross and he was the one standing above them, holding something like verdict and mercy in the same hand.

"You all know what this means," he said finally, and his voice had a softness that did not belong with mercy. "We don't parade this. We don't brag. We let it be. We bury it like it deserves to be buried: quietly, heavy, and done."

They nodded. Some of them swallowed hard. The hush around them felt ceremonial—not religious, not holy—only pure, sober business. K9 stepped up and spat once into the dirt, a small sound like a benediction for the dead who deserved better and the living who didn't.

Cash leaned down and ran his hand over the mound once, slow, like he was closing a book. His fingers picked up mud and it smeared along his knuckles. He didn't wipe it off. He let the stain sit there. It was a token he could carry that meant the world had been changed by a small, furious act and that names could be cleaned or dirtied, depending on who held the shovel.

"Big Apple deserved better," K9 said quietly, and there was something like a sob in the way he spoke. It didn't break Cash, but it hit him in a place he kept shuttered. For a beat, he let himself remember a laugh or a handshake, a story told in the back of a car with the city lights like beads on a prayer.

Cash straightened up. He scanned the horizon—the low-slung apartment blocks, the yellow lights in windows like watching eyes. He thought of how sound carries; he thought of the way the rumor mill would turn and grind and try to turn this into a parable. He thought of the men who had made the choice and the men who would pay the price. He thought of graves and of the small, hollow truth that burying a body didn't bury the thing that started the killing in the first place.

"Walk," he said, and the single word folded the night back into movement. They turned away from the grave and walked back toward the street like a funeral march without music. No one whistled. No one laughed. The city lights welcomed them like spectators at the end of a play.

Once they were a few paces off, Cash stopped and looked back. He watched the earth settle on the new mound and the last line of the day's light slip under the horizon. The story would breathe and shift and be reshaped by mouths that loved a good ending. For now, there was only the dirt and the silence and the private ledger the men had balanced.

Cash breathed in, slow and steady, and let the cool air fill him like a promise and a warning. He had put one thing to rest. He had made a decision that would make enemies and allies in equal measure. He had placed his foot above a grave and, in that single act, told the city what he was willing to do.

They walked on. The night swallowed their footsteps, and the cemetery, patient and old, folded them into its memory like another name on Cash's list of bodies.

Chapter 17

The room smelled like bleach and gunpowder, a mix that clung to the air like bad memories. K9's body was still weak from the bullets, but his rage was stronger than morphine. Curtains were half-drawn, sunlight slipping through like prison bars. K9 sat upright, his eyes cold and half-closed, lost in the storm building inside him.

The door opened slow. Big T stepped in, wearing that same black hoodie he'd had on since the shooting went down. Eyes bloodshot, jaw tight. He'd barely slept. He wasn't coming to check on K9's health; he had something heavier in his pocket, something that could set the streets on fire. He moved quiet, like he didn't want to wake the ghosts that lived in the nights.

K9 didn't speak. He just stared at him, reading his body language like a mirror. Big T nodded once, slow, and said, low, "I got it."

That was all K9 needed to hear.

Big T pulled a small black hard drive from his pocket. He placed it on the table beside the bed, next to K9's gun and his phone. K9's eyes shifted toward it, his jaw tightening. He knew whatever was on there wasn't good; truth never came wrapped in silver.

Big T plugged the drive into the laptop, fingers moving steady. The screen lit up, reflection flashing across both their faces. K9 leaned forward, pain shooting through his ribs, but he didn't care. Big T opened the video file. The footage was shaky at first, caught from a street cam near the block where the ambush happened.

Then it came clear.

A black Cadillac Escalade, bullet holes flashing in the light. K9's car. The one his man was driving that night. The engine idling at the corner, waiting on a call. Then two figures appeared from the shadows. Both masked up, both moving like they'd done this before. One tall, one stocky. They came from the side alley, gloved hands gripping automatics. The tall one—Mac Ru—raised first. Savage was right behind him. The footage caught the muzzle flashes, bright as lightning in the dark.

Bullets tore through the Escalade. The windows exploded, smoke and sparks flying as the truck jerked forward, tires squealing. K9's man never made it a full block before the engine died. The shooters didn't hesitate; they ran back toward a waiting black BMW. The car peeled off, tires screaming against concrete, taillights fading into the dark.

Big T paused the video. Silence filled the room. All that could be heard was the sound of K9 breathing, of the laptop fan.

K9's hands clenched into fists. His knuckles went white, veins standing out like ropes. He leaned back, breathing slow but deep, his face stone. Hate crawled up his chest, heavy and raw. His eyes locked on the frozen image of Mac Ru and Savage on the screen.

Big T stood quiet, letting him process. He'd known K9 long enough to recognize that look—the calm before the hurricane.

K9 didn't say much. His voice came low, more like a growl than words. "These two…" He stopped, jaw flexing. "…they dead motherfuckers."

Big T nodded once, already knowing what was next.

K9 looked back at the screen again, eyes narrowing like a predator sizing up prey. Every frame burned into his memory: the way Mac Ru moved, the way Savage looked around before firing, even the sound of the shots through the cheap security mic. It was all burned in his mind now.

He'd been trying to piece it together since he got hit. He'd doubted Cash. He'd doubted Snake Eyes. But this—this was truth staring him dead in the face. The streets had lied, but the video didn't. And the truth was louder than any rumor.

He slid the laptop off his lap, setting it down slow. His voice broke through the silence again, calm but dripping with venom. "Find them," he said. "I want every corner watched. Every trap. Every hood they ever touched."

Big T nodded again. "Say less."

K9 leaned forward, eyes still fixed on the paused image. His reflection overlapped with the shooters' faces. He almost smiled, but it wasn't from joy; it was the kind of grin that comes right before something terrible. "I'm gonna show them what happens when you fuck with a monster," he muttered, almost to himself.

Big T turned off the video, yanked the drive out, and pocketed it again. He didn't need to ask what came next. Orders didn't need to be spoken when the air was this thick with hate. He knew the move: get the shooters' names back on the block, shake the streets until someone talks, and when they do, bring their location straight to K9. He'd been shot, betrayed, and almost left for dead, but now he had a target. That was all he needed.

Outside the pin house window, the city looked calm, but K9 knew better. The streets were always watching, waiting for the next storm. And when his came, it wasn't gonna be quiet.

He looked down at his bandaged chest, touched the scars lightly, and whispered, "Pain made me." Then his hand slid over to the pistol on the bedside table. He checked the clip, cocked it once, and laid it back down like a promise.

The door clicked open again. His maid peeked in, but the look she saw on his face froze her in place. There was no man in that bed anymore—only a monster waiting for vengeance, waiting for a man's life to be taken.

When she left, the room fell quiet again. The glow from the laptop screen dimmed as the monitor switched to standby. But K9 could still see their faces in his mind—Mac Ru and Savage, laughing somewhere, thinking they got away.

He leaned back, eyes half-closed, replaying every second of the footage in his head. The shots. The smoke. The blood. His man slumped behind the wheel.

This wasn't gonna be business. This was personal.

Big T was already downstairs by then, making calls, lining up cars, whispering to soldiers who didn't ask questions. The city would start shaking by midnight. Everyone who ever breathed the same air as Mac Ru or Savage would feel pressure.

By morning, K9's name would be ringing again louder than before—not as the man recovering from an attempted murder on his life, but as the monster coming back from the dead.

And when he came, there wouldn't be nowhere to hide—just blood and vengeance. Murder and death and bodies dropping, and Mac Ru and Savage names were on the grocery list.

TO BE CONTINUED ...

Lock Down Publications and Ca$h Presents
Assisted Publishing Packages

Due to an increase in the price of services we have increased our prices. The prices below reflect the price increase as of 11/1/24.

BASIC PACKAGE **$699** Editing Cover Design Formatting	**UPGRADED PACKAGE** **$1000** Typing Editing Cover Design Formatting Upload eBooks to Amazon Upload Paperback to Amazon
ADVANCE PACKAGE **$1,400** Typing Editing (line editing/content) Cover Design Formatting Copyright Registration Proofreading Upload eBooks to Amazon Upload Paperback to Amazon	**LDP SUPREME PACKAGE** **$1,700** Typing Editing (line editing/content) Cover Design Formatting Copyright Registration Proofreading Set up Amazon Account Upload eBooks to Amazon Upload Paperback to Amazon Advertise on LDP's Amazon and Facebook Page

***

Other services available upon request.
Additional charges may apply

Lock Down Publications
P.O. Box 944
Stockbridge, GA 30281-9998
Phone: 470 303-9761
Email: lockdownpublications@gmail.com

Submission Guideline

Submit the first three chapters of your completed manuscript to ldpsubmissions@gmail.com. In the subject line add **Your Book's Title**. The manuscript must be in a Word Doc file and sent as an attachment. Document should be in Times New Roman, double spaced, and in size 12 font. Also, provide your synopsis and full contact information. If sending multiple submissions, they must each be in a separate email.

Have a story but no way to send it electronically? You can still submit to LDP/Ca$h Presents. Send in the first three chapters, written or typed, of your completed manuscript to:

LDP: Submissions Dept
P.O. Box 944
Stockbridge, GA 30281-9998

DO NOT send original manuscript. Must be a duplicate. Provide your synopsis and a cover letter containing your full contact information.

Thanks for considering LDP and Ca$h Presents.

NEW RELEASES

BLOODLINE OF A SAVAGE 1-3
THESE VICIOUS STREETS 1-3
RELENTLESS GOON 1-3
BY PRINCE A. TAUHID

THE BUTTERFLY MAFIA 1-3
BY FUMIYA PAYNE

A THUG'S STREET PRINCESS 1&2
BY MEESHA

CITY OF SMOKE 3
BY MOLOTTI

GET IT IN SLUGS 1 &2
BY B. STALL

STANDING ON HER BUSINESS 1&2
BY DG SANTANA

STEPPERS 1,2&3
THE REAL BADDIES OF CHI-RAQ
BY KING RIO

THE LANE 1&2
BY KEN-KEN SPENCE

THUG OF SPADES 1&2
LOVE IN THE TRENCHES 2
CORNER BOYS
BY COREY ROBINSON

TIL DEATH 3
BY ARYANNA

OPPS CRY TOO 3 | SAYNOMORE

THE BIRTH OF A GANGSTER 4
BY DELMONT PLAYER

PRODUCT OF THE STREETS 1-3
BY DEMOND "MONEY" ANDERSON

NO TIME FOR ERROR
BY KEESE

MONEY HUNGRY DEMONS 1-2
BY TRANAY ADAMS

HUB CITY MENACE 1-3
BY J. WHITE

A THUGGISH PASSION 1&2
LAND OF DA HOOLIGANZ 1-4
KILLAZ ON STANDBY 1&2
BY IRA B.

FO'EVA ROLLIN 1&2
BY ASSA RAYMOND BAKER

THE LEVEL UP 1&3
BY LUXURY KING

Coming Soon from Lock Down Publications/Ca$h Presents

IF YOU CROSS ME ONCE 6
ANGEL V
By Anthony Fields

A THUGS STREET PRINCESS 3
By Meesha

CORNER BOYS 2
By Corey Robinson

THA TAKEOVER
By Keith Chandler

BETRAYAL OF A G 2
By Ray Vinci

SAVAGE FAMILY EMPIRE 1&2
SOULLESS GOON 1,2&3
THE DIRTY SIDE OF MONEY 1,2&3
By Prince

FOR MY ENEMY'S SAKE
AMBITIONS OF A SLIDER
FRESH OFF DA PORCH
By IRA B.

BY THE TRUCKLOAD 1-4
TIPPIN' THE SCALES 1-3
BAD BITCHES WIT GUNZ 3
PROBLEM SOLVED 2
By Christopher "Diesel" Hornezes

Available Now

RESTRAINING ORDER 1 & 2
By **CA$H & Coffee**

LOVE KNOWS NO BOUNDARIES 1-3
By **Coffee**

RAISED AS A GOON I, II, III & IV
BRED BY THE SLUMS I, II, III
BLAST FOR ME I & II
ROTTEN TO THE CORE I II III
A BRONX TALE I, II, III
DUFFLE BAG CARTEL I II III IV V VI
HEARTLESS GOON I II III IV V
A SAVAGE DOPEBOY I II
DRUG LORDS I II III
CUTTHROAT MAFIA I II
KING OF THE TRENCHES
By **Ghost**

LAY IT DOWN I & II
LAST OF A DYING BREED I II
BLOOD STAINS OF A SHOTTA I & II III
By **Jamaica**

LOYAL TO THE GAME I II III
LIFE OF SIN I, II III
By **TJ & Jelissa**

IF LOVING HIM IS WRONG…I & II
LOVE ME EVEN WHEN IT HURTS I II III
By **Jelissa**

PUSH IT TO THE LIMIT
By **Bre' Hayes**

BLOODY COMMAS I & II
SKI MASK CARTEL I, II & III
KING OF NEW YORK I II, III IV V
RISE TO POWER I II III
COKE KINGS I II III IV V
BORN HEARTLESS I II III IV
KING OF THE TRAP I II
By **T.J. Edwards**

WHEN THE STREETS CLAP BACK I & II III
THE HEART OF A SAVAGE I II III IV
MONEY MAFIA I II
LOYAL TO THE SOIL I II III
By **Jibril Williams**

A DISTINGUISHED THUG STOLE MY HEART I II & III
LOVE SHOULDN'T HURT I II III IV
RENEGADE BOYS 1-4
PAID IN KARMA 1-3
SAVAGE STORMS 1-3
AN UNFORESEEN LOVE 1-3
BABY, I'M WINTERTIME COLD 1-3
A THUG'S STREET PRINCESS 1&2
By **Meesha**

A GANGSTER'S CODE 1-3
A GANGSTER'S SYN 1-3
THE SAVAGE LIFE 1-3
CHAINED TO THE STREETS 1-3
BLOOD ON THE MONEY 1-3
A GANGSTA'S PAIN 1-3
BEAUTIFUL LIES AND UGLY TRUTHS
CHURCH IN THESE STREETS
By **J-Blunt**

CUM FOR ME 1-8
An LDP Erotica Collaboration

OPPS CRY TOO 3 | SAYNOMORE

BLOOD OF A BOSS 1-5
SHADOWS OF THE GAME
TRAP BASTARD
By **Askari**

THE STREETS BLEED MURDER 1-3
THE HEART OF A GANGSTA 1-3
By **Jerry Jackson**

WHEN A GOOD GIRL GOES BAD
By **Adrienne**

THE COST OF LOYALTY 1-3
By **Kweli**

BRIDE OF A HUSTLA 1-3
THE FETTI GIRLS 1-3
CORRUPTED BY A GANGSTA 1-4
BLINDED BY HIS LOVE
THE PRICE YOU PAY FOR LOVE 1-3
DOPE GIRL MAGIC 1-3
By **Destiny Skai**

A KINGPIN'S AMBITION
A KINGPIN'S AMBITION II
I MURDER FOR THE DOUGH
By **Ambitious**

TRUE SAVAGE 1-7
DOPE BOY MAGIC 1-3
MIDNIGHT CARTEL 1-3
CITY OF KINGZ 1&2
NIGHTMARE ON SILENT AVE
THE PLUG OF LIL MEXICO 1&2
CLASSIC CITY
By **Chris Green**

A GANGSTER'S REVENGE 1-4
THE BOSS MAN'S DAUGHTERS 1-5
A SAVAGE LOVE 1&2
BAE BELONGS TO ME 1&2
A HUSTLER'S DECEIT 1-3
WHAT BAD BITCHES DO 1-3
SOUL OF A MONSTER 1-3
KILL ZONE
A DOPE BOY'S QUEEN 1-3
TIL DEATH 1-3
IMMA DIE BOUT MINE 1-6
DYING FOR LIKES
By **Aryanna**

A DOPEBOY'S PRAYER
By **Eddie "Wolf" Lee**

THE KING CARTEL 1-3
By **Frank Gresham**

THESE NIGGAS AIN'T LOYAL 1-3
By **Nikki Tee**

GANGSTA SHYT 1-3
By **CATO**

THE ULTIMATE BETRAYAL
By **Phoenix**

BOSS'N UP 1-3
By **Royal Nicole**

I LOVE YOU TO DEATH
By **Destiny J**

I RIDE FOR MY HITTA
I STILL RIDE FOR MY HITTA
By **Misty Holt**

LOVE & CHASIN' PAPER
By **Qay Crockett**

TO DIE IN VAIN
SINS OF A HUSTLA
By **ASAD**

BROOKLYN HUSTLAZ
By **Boogsy Morina**

BROOKLYN ON LOCK 1 & 2
By **Sonovia**

GANGSTA CITY
By **Teddy Duke**

A DRUG KING AND HIS DIAMOND 1-3
A DOPEMAN'S RICHES
HER MAN, MINE'S TOO 1&2
CASH MONEY HO'S
THE WIFEY I USED TO BE 1&2
PRETTY GIRLS DO NASTY THINGS
By **Nicole Goosby**

LIPSTICK KILLAH 1-3
CRIME OF PASSION 1-3
FRIEND OR FOE 1-3
By **Mimi**

TRAPHOUSE KING 1-3
KINGPIN KILLAZ 1-3
STREET KINGS 1&2
PAID IN BLOOD 1&2
CARTEL KILLAZ 1-3
DOPE GODS 1&2
By **Hood Rich**

THE STREETS ARE CALLING
By **Duquie Wilson**

STEADY MOBBN' 1-3
THE STREETS STAINED MY SOUL 1-3
By **Marcellus Allen**

WHO SHOT YA 1-3
SON OF A DOPE FIEND 1-4
HEAVEN GOT A GHETTO 1&2
SKI MASK MONEY 1&2
By **Renta**

GORILLAZ IN THE BAY 1-4
TEARS OF A GANGSTA 1/&2
3X KRAZY 1&2
STRAIGHT BEAST MODE 1&2
By **DE'KARI**

TRIGGADALE 1-3
MURDA WAS THE CASE 1-3
By **Elijah R. Freeman**

SLAUGHTER GANG 1-3
RUTHLESS HEART 1-3
By **Willie Slaughter**

GOD BLESS THE TRAPPERS 1-3
THESE SCANDALOUS STREETS 1-3
FEAR MY GANGSTA 1-5
THESE STREETS DON'T LOVE NOBODY 1-2
BURY ME A G 1-5
A GANGSTA'S EMPIRE 1-4
THE DOPEMAN'S BODYGAURD 1&2
THE REALEST KILLAZ 1-3
THE LAST OF THE OGS 1-3
By **Tranay Adams**

MARRIED TO A BOSS 1-3
By **Destiny Skai & Chris Green**

KINGZ OF THE GAME 1-7
CRIME BOSS 1-4
By **Playa Ray**

FUK SHYT
By **Blakk Diamond**

DON'T F#CK WITH MY HEART 1&2
By **Linnea**

ADDICTED TO THE DRAMA 1-3
IN THE ARM OF HIS BOSS
By **Jamila**

LOYALTY AIN'T PROMISED 1&2
By **Keith Williams**

YAYO 1-4
A SHOOTER'S AMBITION 1&2
BRED IN THE GAME
By **S. Allen**

TRAP GOD 1-3
RICH $AVAGE 1-3
MONEY IN THE GRAVE 1-3
CARTEL MONEY 1&2
By **Martell Troublesome Bolden**

FOREVER GANGSTA 1&2
GLOCKS ON SATIN SHEETS 1&2
By **Adrian Dulan**

TOE TAGZ 1-4
LEVELS TO THIS SHYT 1&2
IT'S JUST ME AND YOU
By **Ah'Million**

OPPS CRY TOO 3 | SAYNOMORE

KINGPIN DREAMS 1-3
RAN OFF ON DA PLUG
By **Paper Boi Rari**

THE STREETS MADE ME 1-3
By **Larry D. Wright**

CONFESSIONS OF A GANGSTA 1-4
CONFESSIONS OF A JACKBOY 1-3
CONFESSIONS OF A HITMAN
CONFESSIONS OF A DOPE BOY
By **Nicholas Lock**

I'M NOTHING WITHOUT HIS LOVE
SINS OF A THUG
TO THE THUG I LOVED BEFORE
A GANGSTA SAVED XMAS
IN A HUSTLER I TRUST
By **Monet Dragun**

QUIET MONEY 1-3
THUG LIFE 1-3
EXTENDED CLIP 1&2
A GANGSTA'S PARADISE
By **Trai'Quan**

CAUGHT UP IN THE LIFE 1-3
THE STREETS NEVER LET GO 1-3
By **Robert Baptiste**

NEW TO THE GAME 1-3
MONEY, MURDER & MEMORIES 1-3
By **Malik D. Rice**

CREAM 2-3
THE STREETS WILL TALK
By **Yolanda Moore**

THE STREETS WILL NEVER CLOSE 1-3
By **K'ajji**

LIFE OF A SAVAGE 1-4
A GANGSTA'S QUR'AN 1-4
MURDA SEASON 1-3
GANGLAND CARTEL 1-3
CHI'RAQ GANGSTAS 1-4
KILLERS ON ELM STREET 1-3
JACK BOYZ N DA BRONX 1-3
A DOPEBOY'S DREAM 1-3
JACK BOYS VS DOPE BOYS 1-3
COKE GIRLZ
COKE BOYS
SOSA GANG 1&2
BRONX SAVAGES
BODYMORE KINGPINS
BLOOD OF A GOON
By **Romell Tukes**

CONCRETE KILLA 1-3
VICIOUS LOYALTY 1-3
BLOODY MONEY BAGS
By **Kingpen**

THE ULTIMATE SACRIFICE 1-6
KHADIFI
IF YOU CROSS ME ONCE 1-3
ANGEL 1-4
IN THE BLINK OF AN EYE
By **Anthony Fields**

THE LIFE OF A HOOD STAR
By **Ca$h & Rashia Wilson**

NIGHTMARES OF A HUSTLA 1-3
BLOOD AND GAMES 1&2
By **King Dream**

GHOST MOB
By **Stilloan Robinson**

HARD AND RUTHLESS 1&2
MOB TOWN 251
THE BILLIONAIRE BENTLEYS 1-3
REAL G'S MOVE IN SILENCE
By **Von Diesel**

MOB TIES 1-7
SOUL OF A HUSTLER, HEART OF A KILLER 1-3
GORILLAZ IN THE TRENCHES
OOPS CRY TOO 1&2
THE DAUGHTER OF A CARTEL BOSS
By **SayNoMore**

BODYMORE MURDERLAND 1-3
THE BIRTH OF A GANGSTER 1-4
By **Delmont Player**

FOR THE LOVE OF A BOSS 1&2
By **C. D. Blue**

KILLA KOUNTY 1-5
TENDER
By **Khufu**

MOBBED UP 1-4
THE BRICK MAN 1-5
THE COCAINE PRINCESS 1-10
STEPPERS 1-3
SUPER GREMLIN 1-4
A GANGSTA'S SON
By **King Rio**

MONEY GAME 1&2
By **Smoove Dolla**

OPPS CRY TOO 3 | SAYNOMORE

A GANGSTA'S KARMA 1-5
By **FLAME**

KING OF THE TRENCHES 1-3
By **GHOST & TRANAY ADAMS**

BAD BITCHES WIT GUNZ 1&2
PROBLEM SOLVED
By "Christopher Diesel" Hornezes

QUEEN OF THE ZOO 1&2
By **Black Migo**

GRIMEY WAYS 1-3
BETRAYAL OF A G
By **Ray Vinci**

XMAS WITH AN ATL SHOOTER
By **Ca$h & Destiny Skai**

KING KILLA 1&2
By **Vincent "Vitto" Holloway**

BETRAYAL OF A THUG 1&2
By **Fre$h**

COUNTDOWN OF A KILLA 1&2
SEX, MURDER AND GOD 1&2
GUNS DOWN, BOTTOMS UP 1&2
By Lo-Life

THE MURDER QUEENS 1-7
By **Michael Gallon**

FOR THE LOVE OF BLOOD 1-4
By **Jamel Mitchell**

OPPS CRY TOO 3 | SAYNOMORE

HOOD CONSIGLIERE 1&2
NO TIME FOR ERROR
By **Keese**

PROTÉGÉ OF A LEGEND 1,2&3
LOVE IN THE TRENCHES 1&2
By **Corey Robinson**

THE PLUG'S RUTHLESS DAUGHTER 1&2
By **Tony Daniels**

BORN IN THE GRAVE 1-3
CRIME PAYS
By **Self Made Tay**

MOAN IN MY MOUTH
By **XTASY**

TORN BETWEEN A GANGSTER AND A GENTLEMAN
By **J-BLUNT & Miss Kim**

LOYALTY IS EVERYTHING 1-3
CITY OF SMOKE 1-3
By **Molotti**

HERE TODAY GONE TOMORROW 1&2
By **Fly Rock**

WOMEN LIE MEN LIE 1-4
FIFTY SHADES OF SNOW 1-3
STACK BEFORE YOU SPLURGE
GIRLS FALL LIKE DOMINOES
NAÏVE TO THE STREETS
By **ROY MILLIGAN**

PILLOW PRINCESS
By **S. Hawkins**

OPPS CRY TOO 3 | SAYNOMORE

THE BUTTERFLY MAFIA 1-3
SALUTE MY SAVAGERY 1&2
By **Fumiya Payne**

THE LANE 1&2
By Ken-Ken Spence

THE PUSSY TRAP 1-5
By **Nene Capri**

DIRTY DNA
By **Blaque**

SANCTIFIED AND HORNY
by **XTASY**

BOOKS BY LDP'S CEO, CA$H

TRUST IN NO MAN
TRUST IN NO MAN 2
TRUST IN NO MAN 3
BONDED BY BLOOD
SHORTY GOT A THUG
THUGS CRY
THUGS CRY 2
THUGS CRY 3
TRUST NO BITCH
TRUST NO BITCH 2
TRUST NO BITCH 3
TIL MY CASKET DROPS
RESTRAINING ORDER
RESTRAINING ORDER 2
IN LOVE WITH A CONVICT
LIFE OF A HOOD STAR
XMAS WITH AN ATL SHOOTER

www.ingramcontent.com/pod-product-compliance
Lightning Source LLC
LaVergne TN
LVHW010920110826
845149LV00013B/2430

9781971770086